LAURA

Summer

of

No

Rain

Summer of No Rain - Copyright 2022 © Laura Hunter & Bluewater Publications
First Edition
ISBN 978-1-949711-82-0 Paper Trade
ISBN 978-1-949711-83-7 eBook
ISBN 978-1-949711-91-2 Audio

Library of Congress Control Number: 2021945300

Bluewater Publications
Bwpublications.com
Printed in the United States

This work is based on the author's personal research, perspective and imagination.

Cover Design – Sierra Tabor
Editor – Sierra Tabor
Interior Design – Rachel Davis
Managing Editor – Angela Broyles

Endorsements for *Summer of No Rain*

"From the opening line, Hunter's sure hand swept me into this story of the summer of 1968 in southwest Alabama, weaving a forgotten piece of our past with the rustle of dried corn husks, the taste of sweat, and the burn of a deep wrong. Poignant and beautifully sculpted with hard truths that sit as dry as a land parched from a summer of no rain, this is a story that will stay with you long after the last page."

> — T. K. Thorne, author of *Behind the Magic Cutain: Secrets, Spies, and Unsung White Allies of Birmingham's Civil Rights Days*

"Laura Hunter writes with a poet's hand, beckoning her readers to Hyssop, Alabama, where purple martins get drunk on chinaberries and Margaret Ann Odom, an innocent young Black girl, becomes an unwilling participant in a shocking eugenics experiment. Told with compassion and respect, *Summer of No Rain* takes readers to a time and place that seems distant yet contemporary, encouraging us to examine our own culpability in America's ongoing racial discord."

> — Ruth Pettey Jones, author of *Chicken Soup for the Soul*

"Although this story inflicts horror, sadness, and pain as surely as the injections given to Margaret Ann, this multi-award-winning author has woven a powerful plot pulsing with characters so real the reader can almost taste the summer's dust."

> — Carolyn Breckinridge (Ezell), author, recipient of Druid City Arts Award for Literature, and retired Clinical Social Worker

"Laura Hunter captured an incredible amount of vibrancy with her stellar Southern writing style and voice...With a fictional pen based on true events, the covers are pulled back to reveal the sick plans those on the wrong side of history had for women who didn't either make the race or socio-economic grade. Furthermore, it's a cautionary tale of how people can rationalize their actions to blind their own conscious to the truth and move forward in insidious plans for a vulnerable group."

— LaMonique Mac, author of The Mixed Girl Series

"In *Summer of No Rain*, Laura Hunter bravely delves into an ugly chapter of Alabama and Southern racial history...The story she tells is inherently powerful, but what makes this story even more powerful is Hunter's rare ability with language and her beautiful rendering of the character Margaret Ann, who suffers what she should never have had to suffer. Hunter lets young Margaret Ann tell her own story, and because she does so, our empathy and outrage are made palpable in the way great fiction can achieve."

— Marlin Barton, author of *Children of Dust* and *Pasture Art*

"Laura Hunter has vividly recreated a childhood world in the waning days of Jim Crow, where cynicism instead of nostalgia rules."

— M. E. Hubbs, author of *The Secret of Wattensaw Bayou*

Disclaimer

Summer of No Rain is a work of fiction based on historical fact. Certain long-standing institutions, agencies, and public offices are mentioned, and the occurring events are based on actual happenings. With the exception of public figures, any resemblance to persons living or dead is coincidental. The opinions expressed are those of the characters and should not be confused with the author's or the publisher's views.

Purge me with hyssop, and I shall be clean: wash me, and I shall be whiter than snow.

Psalm 51:7 KJV

Part I

Chapter 1

July, 1968

That first day, Nurse opened the door to the examination room as if she had some black magic tell her I was there. She had a surgical mask over her nose and mouth. Fact is, if she ever smiled, I never saw it. I never saw her without that white mask. She was tall with graying hair in tight curls and dressed in white from her cap to her white stockings and shoes. She moved like a machine that needed oil. Her metal-gray eyes darted from side to side as if she was looking for somebody else. When her eyes settled on me, she motioned me inside with her index finger. My first thought was that I had done something bad.

A child led by a grown-up doesn't question. I'd been brought up right. I could have argued that I had been good, that I didn't need Nurse's crooked finger, but nobody gave me a chance to say anything. I couldn't recall a time when I broke one of Brother Blues' commandants on purpose, and I always obeyed M'dear. I meant to be good.

Later on, I would ask myself if I had been sent to the clinic because I'd been bad. At school, other girls' arms didn't have shot marks. If someone had asked me to say a time when I had a flicker of suspicion about the clinic, I would say it happened when I looked for marks on other kids and never found a single one.

Once inside the treatment room, I shivered, though the heat outside had smothered me. Everything in the room was either cold steel or hard white. It all looked expensive and important. It had that closed-off smell that comes from leaving the barn door locked for too long. An almost moldy stink that comes from too little fresh air. You remember it because it gets locked up in your nose and you can't get it out.

The dim light made it hard to see. The room's four windows had been boarded up across the bottom, but each had space at the top, too little for a kid to climb through. Three had brown paper shades pulled part way down. The other windowpane had been broken at some point, and it had a little orange pillow stuffed in it to keep out the sun. Time and neglect had left rain-streaked lines of dirt down each pane. A pale light came from a bulb under a dust-covered metal shade in the middle of the room. Cone-shaped, it hung over a flat table.

A dingy sheet dragged over the table on one side and puddled on the plank floor. The table had two bent scoops at the end. They reminded me of metal dippers with stirrups for feet. They reached toward the ceiling, as if an unnamed something up there wanted my attention. I looked up. For a heartbeat, a flicker of white moved across the ceiling. I blinked and looked again, but nothing was there. All I saw were spiderwebs that filled each ceiling corner. I waited for a spider to drop down and web-up the lone fly that buzzed around the room, but it never happened.

Across from the door was another door, with its metal painted gray like the first. It had a padlock threaded through two thick C-shaped hasps. I opened and closed my mouth, searching for words that would let me out of the room. I found not a single one.

Nurse went to one of the shiny carts. In a thick-walled glass jar stood several syringes. Their needles' tips rested in a dry brown stain on the square jar's bottom. The same brown as the wooden walls. *Somebody's used that jar as a coffee cup*, I thought. Nurse took out a syringe, filled it with a clear liquid, and laid it on the table. Just then, Dr. Graves called her into the next room. Miss Claire, the White lady who had brought me to the clinic, had told me Dr. Graves would be there. He was "esteemed," she had said, and she was proud to work with him.

Parts of the room reminded me of a kitchen. A percolator sat on the counter by a small, boxy refrigerator, empty medicine bottles had been left out by a one-eyed hot plate, and two coffee mugs waited for somebody to fill one.

With Nurse gone, I edged over to the cart. I picked up the medicine vial. A little circle without dust marked where it had set. I shook it. It moved like the white Karo syrup M'dear poured on my pancakes. Thick. *It'll have a hard time getting into my arm*, my brain said. I put it back inside its clean circle.

Beside the medicine sat a box of different needles, all sizes. They looked like those Mr. Gibbons used for sick cattle. A tiny peephole opened in my brain and a little question flew out. *Am I getting heifer medicine?* I held my breath. *Surely not.*

"Stainless Steel Hypodermic Needles" was printed across the top of the box. I picked up the top. Words on the edge said "Veterinary Type." Nurse had chosen the biggest for me. *She must be giving me heifer medicine.* No matter. Medicine was medicine. I couldn't speak up. I couldn't get out. I didn't really care. I didn't want to be there, but I had no choice. This was M'dear's plan, not mine.

I lifted the syringe Nurse had left out on the counter. At first, its weight surprised me, but having seen Mr. Gibbons with the cattle, I laughed at my silly self. Of course it would be heavy. It had metal wings on each side so Nurse could push out the air and suck up the medicine. The slanted metal point would let the tip prick the skin. It was large enough to draw blood. I cringed as I thought about what was to come.

Nurse came back into the room, quiet as a mouse in her rubber-soled shoes. She eyed me hard from over her mask. *Did she think I was going to steal her needle?*

"You people," she mumbled through her mask and shook her head.

What people is she talking about? I was the only one there. I bit my lip and moved back to the covered table.

She squirted the syrupy liquid into the air. It settled on the floor. Could've been a glob of spit. "Drop your pants."

There it was. My fear put into words. I lifted my skirt and lowered my underpants. I bent over the table and gripped its opposite side with both hands. This would hurt. Nurse jabbed in the needle. I gasped as hot pain from the medicine spread through my hip. I felt the syringe's weight pull it to one side. I gritted my teeth and held the table harder, so as not to grab the needle and yank it out. It burned all through my muscle. Silent tears dropped on the sheet. Nurse pulled out the needle and slapped my hip hard. She kneaded my flesh as if it was tough biscuit dough. If she was trying to make the pain go away, she didn't.

I pulled up my underpants and dropped my skirt. Nurse nodded toward the door. Maybe I was supposed to thank her. I opened my mouth to speak, but when I saw her eyebrows close in on each other, I changed my mind and walked out. When I got home, I had a smear of blood on my underpants, but I rinsed it out before M'dear saw.

Chapter 2

The summer of 1968 hovers over me like some faceless ghost. Not a true spirit like Bailey Renfroe's, but a ghost that holds me tight like a captured runaway. Fifty years now, and it's still here.

I don't look quite white. My complexion is a dusky color, a little like honey. When I went north, I might could've passed. Not that M'dear wanted me to try to pass. She just wanted me to have a better life than she did. I'm mulatto. That's colored. That won't change. I find myself checking this pock scar on my right jaw with my finger, thinking that one day it'll disappear. It hasn't. It won't.

Life had been simple for me and M'dear. Then Miss Claire Whitehurst, a social worker from the Free Women's Clinic, came. It was July 22nd, a

Monday. I remember because M'dear marked the kitchen calendar with a star. "Important day," she said. You would have thought it was a holiday. Me, Margaret Ann Odom, one of the first girls to go to the new Free Women's Clinic. She seemed real proud.

After all these years, the story's still told here in my hometown of Sweetwater, Alabama. People tell it different ways, but I know better than anybody what the truth is. It's my story. It changed my life. I was twelve. I'm sixty-two now, and folks here think I ought to have married, but I don't know. No man wants an empty vessel. During the years I lived with Brother Blues' sister, Miss Paulette, we never talked about it. Not the needles. Not the shots. Not the sores. It's the fact that I didn't matter that haunts me. It took me a long time to understand what the shots had been for and what it meant for me. And my daddy? I know now what he did, but even more hurtful was what he didn't do.

That summer of 1968 was hot, hotter than anybody could remember. I thought I would die. The community of Hyssop calls that time the summer of no rain. By mid-July, all that had greened out in spring had turned burnt brown. The crop-duster, who flew over the area to check the drought, hadn't heard of the few houses and stores called Hyssop. He came to see if drought had killed the hyssop, he said. He meant hyssop the plant. When healthy and in bloom, the fields around Sweetwater look like a velvet covering has dropped from the sky and hid the land. Hyssop the plant drew people in off the highway just to look. The land lay covered in purple blooms, their stamens tipped in blood red. Our fields look otherworldly.

Sometimes, Brother Blues talks about hyssop in the Bible and reads its praises in Psalms. It has healing power. Blooms that look like gentle little faces each with seedpods alongside it, barely open, as if tempting an insect to come inside and explore. But this scene was not what the pilot saw. Instead, he said the place looked "wounded, as if it was trying to form a brown scab over the ground." He saw the land's famine and wondered how people could live here. He saw our little gray house and my chinaberry tree. Even the chinaberries had shriveled early and threatened to drop.

The chinaberry tree outside my window was my hiding place. From the top of the chinaberry, I could see all of the countryside. The pilot had been right. Sweetwater and all around looked dead. Chinaberry trees are made for climbing. Any kid knows that. It's big enough to shade the south side of our house. Most of the day, the house sits in its shadow. It's got a thick limb that grows so close to my window that I could climb out and be in the top, hidden by large leaves before M'dear missed me. It's perfect for spying.

Me and M'dear lived at the end of the road, inside the pasture, surrounded by Hank Bullard's black angus. It was a good way out and M'dear never drove. I walked the dirt road from our house to Brother Blues Marshall's store and back. That's where I would go, mostly, except to Gladstone Industrial and Trade School north of Hyssop. A thin wire fence around the house and chinaberry tree keeps cattle out of our vegetable garden and front yard. And it keeps the hens close to the house. A longer, higher fence that goes out of sight surrounds the pasture. The only fence opening to the outside I know of is the cattle guard about a hundred yards from our gate.

Drive three miles west and cross a line as invisible as gravity. A sign announces the shift in place. A wooden sign with the name "Hyssop" etched and filled with charcoal tells what few travelers that might appear on our road where they are. Knee-high grass rustles around the two-by-fours that hold the sign up. During that summer, not a breeze passed through Hyssop without raising sounds like crisp cornhusks.

Ours was not a town in the true sense of the word, but a section of the county settled in 1879 by freed slaves. They created a bulge in the road and grew sugarcane and cotton on Buckhorn River's black bottomland so deep in its richness that what it grew was sweeter than sugar. Larger than life even.

Hyssop had two and a half buildings: Blues Marshall's General Store and Eb Hawkins' Barber Shop and Surgery. In Mr. Eb's front window are two hand-lettered signs in red: "We pull teeth" and "We bind wounds." Another building is gradually falling in. Its roof caved in years ago. It had been a weigh station for cotton, now no more than a wooden shack, sinking day by day deeper into the ground. For a time, it stood like a shrine to backs bent from picking cotton from dawn until dusk. "You done a good job." that weigh station once said. Now nothing around here says so.

Old men gather on Eb's porch and gaze across at what's left. They debate who brought in the most cotton to be weighed and who left with the least money in their overall pockets. They argue what day and how many years ago it has been. Every man has his own story. None of the stories match. As far as I know, no one will ever take an ax to the wood. The weigh station is no more than a skeleton of what it was.

I spent my growing-up summers going and coming from Brother Blues' store. He pampered me like his own, as he had known M'dear since my daddy first set her down in Hyssop. He recalls the first time, twelve years earlier, when M'dear brought me to preaching and how beautiful M'dear was, sitting up there on full sweet feed sacks and cradling me in her arms. He says she sat up there so she could see him over everybody else.

"Looked like a African queen," he says. "Her thick hair with a sweet shrub bloom tucked behind her ear. No need for a fancy Sunday hat."

He tells me all the time about that Sunday and ends every time with a stout chuckle. He says I "growed beautiful"—that's his words—and I love him for saying it.

I got M'dear's high Cherokee cheekbones, long, thick black hair with "just enough wave to make White women and coloreds alike jealous." M'dear laughs when she says that. My hair refuses to kink up as much as the other girls' in school. No amount of Royal Crown Hair Dressing can make it so. My skin felt so soft and smooth then, before the shots. To wake me in the mornings, M'dear would rub her fingertips down my cheeks. "My baby," M'dear would say. "Put you in a brood of newborn chicks and you'll be the golden one, touched with a hint of brown." M'dear could have been some kind of poet had she got to go to school.

Chapter 3

It was one of those days early in July that me and M'dear first met Miss Claire, before the Clinic visits began. I sat across at the kitchen table from where M'dear ironed. She moved away from her ironing board and wiped sweat from her face with a dishrag. Other than the heat, today was a day like any other day with M'dear trying to hold on to what she had. A place to lay our heads, enough food not to starve, and enough juice to feed her iron.

Outside, a quiet swishing sound, much like a hushed wind, blew in the window over the sink. A shadow flickered. Something dark and thick had dropped outside. I jumped up. M'dear stopped ironing and slid out of her brown corduroy mules. She stepped out the back door to look for the possibility of rain. I followed her, like a silent ghost.

It wasn't a cloud of dust, but a noise of quivers. It wasn't a building wind, but a massive flock of purple martins, their color so intense they looked black. The flock soared up in a whirlwind of flapping wings thick enough to hide the sky. Then something within their core told them to separate. One side moved east toward the low hills north of the cattle pasture. The other wedge settled in my chinaberry tree.

Within minutes, birds began to fall from the tree. Each landed with a *plunk*, one after another. M'dear gathered her full, flowery smock under her bosom. She held it tight against her body to absorb her sweat, something she always did. Standing next to her in the door, I could smell her musk. Her scent took me back to damp leaves in the fall. I thought about how long ago fall seemed.

Outside, the ground around us glowed black. Bird after bird plopped from the chinaberry tree and lay dark in the dirt. Across the yard, a martin, trying to lift itself, shook one wing, as if waving at us. After several tries, the bird righted itself, stood for a moment on wobbly legs then dived forward. Its black beak speared the ground. Near the step, a martin shuddered as if in pain. Another thrashed about as if possessed by some old demon.

M'dear sat on the top step while we watched. I knelt and massaged her swollen feet. She spread her toes for a little relief. "What's happening to them?" I asked.

"Fed on them chinaberries. Ever' one's crazy drunk."

"That the way of such a bird?"

"Oh, they'll recover and take to the sky again. And most likely come back to feed." She smiled. "All God's creatures, they got they own way. Got they own place even if they can't always make sense of it."

That July day while we watched the drunk birds, M'dear gave up on them having any sense and stepped back inside. "All they good for's to stir up dust." She wiped her lips. "Taste that dirt, Sugar Baby? This whole world needs a good, cleansing rain."

I could feel sand on my lips. It did taste like dirt.

Brother Blues called M'dear a mere mite of a woman. She had always been tiny. Tiny bones, tiny feet. Her puffed hair looked more like a black halo than a polished do. Struggled all her life. A mighty task for a slight woman. From the beginning, she meant for me to have a job with authority. M'dear ironed every day but Sunday, from can to can't, but ironing wasn't her life. Ironing was her planning time. While she ironed, she planned my life, sometimes talking out loud to herself. That made it true, saying it out loud.

I once asked her where she got such a fancy name as Margaret Ann for such an ordinary girl as me. When she was a child, she said her mama took her into Eufaula in South Alabama where they lived to let a dentist pull a tooth that paregoric wasn't soothing.

"Was this woman there who had her name carved in a piece of wood on her desk. When I asked my mama what did it say, she whispered the words to me. 'Margaret Ann Fields.' She was pudgy in just the right places to please her man." M'dear talked with a grin in her voice.

"M'dear, don't say that."

Gazing across the pasture, she sat up taller and kept on talking, like somebody was there I couldn't see. "Had hair gelled to her scalp in deep waves. She had to have used half a jar of Liv

Crème Hairdressing on her head. Surprised she didn't have grease dripping off her forehead. Not three-sixty waves like the brothers wore. Them ropes that wrapped around they heads, but waves like a White woman would have had in the 20s. And her hands. Perfect hands that danced over black letter keys. She had on a two-piece suit, the deepest green you ever did see, with big pearl buttons down the front. Oh how I wanted to brush my hand over that suit."

M'dear continued, "From time to time, I peeped up to watch the woman's fingers chase each other across the typewriter, until my mama slapped my leg and told me to quit being nosey." M'dear let out a heavy, longing sigh. "I think of that suit ever' time I see the hyssop with its glossy green leaves growing around here."

After M'dear had her own girl-child—that's me—she decided that I would type on a typewriter and have polished fingernails and wear bought suits to work every day. I would sit wherever on the city bus, whenever I wanted, thanks to Mrs. Rosa Parks. I would go back to Gladstone County Industrial and Training School in early August and get learning that would keep me in a life far removed from living in a house surrounded by cattle dung and chicken poop.

As I got older, M'dear fed me platters of her ambition as often as she fed me greens and corn-pone. She told me I was free. Free to ride the bus, free to walk the White man's road, free to live in peace, but she lied. It was her truth because she said it. It could be a lie to everybody else, but not to her. She lied because she didn't know any different.

It was on that morning of the drunk birds that Claire Whitehurst showed up in our lives.

Somebody tapped on the front screen door midday. "Get off that chair, Sugar Baby. Somebody's here."

I dashed to the screen door. A bright green Jeepster Commando was parked at the gate, its white top gleaming in the sun. I could see not one speck of dirt on it anywhere. It must have dropped out of the sky and settled without stirring up one dust devil. A woman stepped into my vision. With the sun behind her, the woman was no more than a shadow.

"Morning, Miss Odom." Her voice said she was young, maybe not much older than M'dear had been when she moved into this house. Her pronunciation said "White."

I squinted because of the sun, and there was M'dear right behind me. She stepped forward. She put her hand on the screen's latch to hold it closed, if the stranger tried to come in. To see her plain, we would have to go out on the porch.

"I'm Ophelia." M'dear tilted her head to get a better look. "Ophelia Odom." Up close, all we could tell was that the woman wore a little yellow hat shaped like a round box. She wore it like it wasn't there, like somebody had set it on top of her head without her noticing. "How come you know my name?"

"May I come in?" the woman asked. "I'd like to talk to you about your daughter."

I ducked behind M'dear.

"Ain't meaning to be disrespecting you none, but I don't know you, and I don't know how you know me or my kin." M'dear grasped the door with her other hand, in case she needed to shut it quick. She could be feisty if she needed to.

"Claire Whitehurst." She stuck out her hand, but M'dear didn't turn loose the door. "I'm with the Free Women's Clinic." The woman watched the floor as if she expected a roach to crawl over her shoe. "It's a clinic that's been opened near here as a part of the Civil Rights Bill. The one signed by former President Johnson. 1964." She hesitated. "I'm sure you know about it."

M'dear didn't react. She spoke to me out of the side of her mouth. "Get back in there and turn off my iron before it scorches the board cover."

M'dear later recalled that she wasn't sure if Claire Whitehurst meant the clinic was free or if it was for free women. Maybe this was what Brother Blues meant when he preached on changing times. But this President Johnson, a White man, why would he set up clinics for people he don't know? And free? For coloreds? M'dear and me, we had talked grown-up things. I was well into my twelfth year. M'dear's life had trained her in the art of expecting the worst, and I lived off her vision. She survived by questioning more often than accepting.

We had studied about the presidents last year when I was in the fourth grade, but I didn't remember much. The last president M'dear remembered up close had been shot by some Communist in Texas, but that was about the time all the Bull Connor and George Wallace riots happened.

"If I'd had my say, I'd let the Reverend King be president. Brother Blues's mighty high on him. And he was a preacher too. But Reverend King was shot dead a couple years back by the government, claimed most," M'dear told me.

With all this happening and what had happened in "Bombingham," killing those little Black girls a couple of summers ago, our people lived under the same pall as the Israelites under Ahab until Elijah took Jezebel down with the rabid dogs. That's what Brother Blues preached. I scurried back to the screen door.

"Do you mind if I come in?" Claire Whitehurst stepped back from the door. "Or might you come out? I'm here to talk to you about health services at the clinic."

"How you know so much about me and mines?" M'dear stuck out her chin. I had seen that move before. It appeared whenever M'dear dared me to "try doing that one more time."

"Census reports. Part of my job. I research all the people who qualify for services, and I found that your Margaret Ann is the right age to begin."

"Give me a minute." M'dear stepped into the kitchen, slid her feet into her flattened mules, and unplugged her iron, even though I had turned it off.

Back on the porch, M'dear cracked open the screen. The White woman hadn't moved. "My Margaret Ann, she ain't had no health program, but she ain't had no health problems neither. Other than colds and once she had a bout of measles, but the teachers put all the children in the same room for a couple of days so they could get the measles together."

M'dear stepped out of the house. I followed her like a dogged shadow. She motioned for the White woman to sit in the rocker. The woman sat. M'dear took the ladder-back chair for herself once the White woman settled. I leaned against the wall.

"Our goal is to prevent Margaret Ann from having any medical issues." Claire Whitehurst sat with both feet flat on the floor, her back straight. "Preventative medicine, it's called." She wore black shoes with short thin heels and stockings despite the July heat.

I looked down at my naked foot. Dirt had buried itself under my big toenail. Her yellow dress showed wet under the arms. The woman held what looked like a flat black pocketbook on her lap with both hands.

She offered to come by and take me to the Clinic for inoculations to keep me healthy. A shot, maybe two times a week at first, then once a week, at no cost to M'dear. Claire Whitehurst herself would pick me up and bring me home, and it was just down the road, so it wouldn't take much time at all. "I'll see that Margaret Ann's safe and in good hands at all times," Miss Whitehurst promised.

I didn't like this plan at all. Shots every week or more? Why me?

M'dear listened. Inside a puff of hot air caught a door and it slammed. The White woman jumped. Papers spilled out of her pocketbook and slid cross the porch like uncooked rice. I picked them up and handed them back to her. She slid them into the pocketbook. "Thank you." She looked me in the eye and smiled. I didn't smile back.

Claire Whitehurst talked. M'dear listened. Words bounced about the porch I'd never heard. Words like "equal application," "public accommodations," "equal protection under the Twelfth Amendment" or something like that. M'dear nodded her head and I nodded mine. The only word I recognized had been "discrimination." Brother Blues talked discrimination almost every Sunday, but I had never seen how that affected me or M'dear. Not out here at the edge of Sweetwater. M'dear didn't know about amendments. I didn't know much. At the edge of the porch, a breeze picked up a dust devil and danced it across the yard.

I knew M'dear. By nodding her head, she hoped the woman believed she understood, so I did the same. Otherwise, she might pass on me because my mama was ignorant. "All you have to do is sign this paper. It says that Margaret Ann can go to the clinic once a week or more and receive treatments as designated by the doctor in charge. That would be Dr. Graves. He's an esteemed specialist from North Carolina." She waited for M'dear to speak. "That's exactly what it says, Miss Odom," Claire Whitehurst promised. "Go to the clinic once a week or more and receive treatments as designated by the doctor in charge."

The breeze died. The dust devil collapsed.

I recalled a story M'dear had told me about her own mother. Before she worked the house for Mrs. Bullard in Eufaula, she took in washing to feed her family. Bent over a footed iron pot set in a scorching fire, her do-rag binding her hair, her mama scrubbed White people's clothes with lye soap, in summer heat and winter cold. Steam boiled up and around and kinked the gray-speckled hair that escaped her triangular scrap of cloth. I imagined my grandmother's scratchy hands as they tugged at M'dear's pigtail and tightened its string bow. She bundled them in rags to keep their bloody cracks from staining the quilt at night. No. I could tell. For M'dear, there was no thinking this out.

M'dear asked where. The woman pointed. M'dear marked her "X" under the heavy black line. The next morning, Miss Claire picked me up in the green Jeep with the bright white top and drove me to the Free Women's Clinic.

Chapter 4

The idea of riding in a car made me shiver. I had ridden the school bus for six years. It held so many kids that one bus could fill two classrooms. Space to move around enticed kids to ignore the driver's commands to stay put, and instead we walked up and down the aisle. It moved like a slug, tossing us into the air whenever its tires rolled over holes in the road.

Riding the school bus was like being in a moving room that took me from Brother Blues' store porch to the double front doors of a cinder block building. The sign above the doors had once read "Gladstone County Industrial and Training School." Several letters were now missing, making the name an unrecognizable jumble of letters.

I would be riding in a car, not to school, but to a women's clinic. "You'll be riding high cotton,"

M'dear said with laughter in her voice.

M'dear had expected me to be excited about going to the clinic in a bright new car, so my scrunched brow and questions surprised her. How would I get home? Was M'dear going with me? What was I supposed to talk about with this White woman? My questions spilled out like unused buttons from an upended dresser drawer.

"Cars is better than a old school bus," M'dear told me.

"But I'll be with a White woman," I countered.

"You going to the new clinic so's you can be healthy."

"To a doctor I never heard of?"

"Yous twelve years old. You got to learn to talk to White womens," M'dear said. "And leave that ratty old lamb doll home."

I dropped my toy lamb, Baa, on the couch. "Maybe I won't talk at all," I mumbled. I would just answer questions. I could answer questions. I did it all the time at school.

Why did this White woman think I wasn't healthy? I thought I was healthy. I hadn't had my monthlies yet, but I'd heard girls at school talk. Some had. Some hadn't. "This about my monthlies?" I cut my eyes under my brows to glance at my mother.

"Not necessarily." M'dear took a deep breath. "You near to being a young woman. Here you goes asking questions like a little child." She turned her back to me. "Set your mind to it. You going."

I might as well face it. M'dear wanted me to go to the clinic. I stepped out the door and waited in the heat. At least, I didn't have to walk half a mile to catch the ride. The car was coming to my house.

I saw the dust cloud before I saw the Jeepster. As it drew closer, the Jeepster Commando looked like it had been shrunk in a hot wash when compared to the size of the yellow school bus. The Jeepster bumped over the cattle guard that separated the pasture from the road. It settled down on the strip of gravel that led to the front porch. Dust made ready by six weeks of drought puffed up behind it. Dead air made the dust slow to fall back in place.

The Jeepster was bright green with a white top the color of an old man's hair. Its tires, though thick and heavy, were so much smaller than bus tires. Still shiny with their newness, the whitewalls reflected the sun's glare.

I dashed back inside and grabbed my lamb. I stuffed Baa in my pocket and stepped off the porch when Miss Whitehurst stopped the Jeepster. Brutal afternoon heat muffled my steps. I walked up to the Jeepster and ran my hand over the fender. Its slickness surprised me. The bus fenders felt rough, pocked with rust holes. I peered under the fender. It was no thicker than my fingernail. The words "beautiful, but dangerous" shouted from every inch of the Jeepster. I saw no joy in getting into what seemed to be little more than a painted tin bucket on wheels.

Miss Claire reached across to the passenger door and motioned me in. I slid over the leather and gripped the seat's edge with both hands. I sat with my head angled toward the dashboard. She told me I could call her Claire.

I knew better than to fall for that trap. Miss Claire maybe, but no colored girl called a White woman by her first name. Not in Alabama. I looked at her long fingers, the nails polished a baby pink. Claire Whitehurst wore no rings or bracelets. Maybe she was poor, but probably not. A new car wasn't a poor man's car, and Claire Whitehurst wore a bought dress, orange with white strips, made from a cloth I didn't know. It looked thick and hot. But her smile was friendly.

"Buckle your seatbelt, and we're off," she said.

Miss Claire sounded so easy. I looked around for a belt. I didn't see one.

"Here. Scooch up." Miss Claire reached behind me and grasped the strip of fabric that dangled next to the door. "You're my first client, you know."

I took the belt and laid it across my legs.

Miss Claire chuckled. "Never used a seatbelt? Click the end into this slot." She tugged. "What's that in your pocket?"

"My lamb." I sat still until I heard the click. "What's it for?"

"A new safety feature to hold you in place." Miss Claire tugged the end so that the waist belt held me secure. "If there's a wreck."

I caught my breath. I knew this little Jeepster wasn't safe. "Do we have to go in this car?"

"It's all we got." Miss Claire looked at me sideways as she cranked the motor. "Have you never been in a car before?"

"Just a school bus. It's big. Not no little tin can like this."

"This Jeepster is going to take us to places neither of us has ever known before." She patted my leg. "Just you wait and see." She put the gear in reverse and turned back to cross the cattle guard. I took my stiff-legged lamb from my pocket and held it tight in both hands.

As we drove past Blues Marshall's General Store, I ducked my head. I had dreaded the going, but M'dear told me I had to go. Said she'd talked it over with Brother Blues and it seemed right that now something was happening to help us coloreds. This free clinic would keep me from getting sick like poor coloreds over past Hyssop. Doctors had come up with shots—"vaccines," she said they were called—that would keep me from getting measles and mumps and scarlet fever and smallpox and sore throats. I'd be healthy as a cow.

So I went. We rode toward Sweetwater until we came to a new road. It was no more than a strip scraped out of dirt. The clinic sat a good ways off the main road. Fire ants had loosened dirt into pyramids around poles the power company had set up to bring in electricity. The road was so narrow that scratchy weeds bent and broke as the

Jeepster moved past them, and a rooster trail of dust followed us.

No signs said where to turn. Miss Claire drove on her own knowing. At the end of the road, there was the old three-room WPA school that had closed in the 1950s when the Whites got a new school in Sweetwater. The only building on the road, it had to be the Free Women's Clinic. From the front wall, an air conditioner stuck out the bottom part of a window. The place had one front door, which we passed, and one side door. I expected to see the word "Colored" over the door, but there was no sign. Nothing. Miss Claire stopped.

"We not going to the back door?"

Miss Claire shook her head. "No back doors here. You go in. Get your shot, and we'll be on our way." She slammed the passenger door behind me. Her brown hair swayed. She had that Jackie Kennedy haircut with just a whisper of bangs, but hers moved around a lot more.

Too strange, I thought, *not having a back door for coloreds*. I knew from Brother Blues that White policemen had attacked people in a church up in Tuscaloosa. They were planning a march about having a water fountain marked "Coloreds Only" in the new courthouse after the Whites promised not. But that was miles and miles north from here. I didn't see how that had a bearing on me.

Miss Claire stepped into the brittle grass. It crunched like a heifer chewing dry hay. I stared off into space, not looking at the door. I ought to be home in my tree house, not at this place. Rats or snakes or ghosts, anything could be in there. Miss Claire pushed me from the back, so I moved on.

Somebody had stacked up concrete blocks, too wobbly for steps. Scary, but we didn't fall. Inside, three rooms had signs that said what they were. "Office," "Examination," and "Treatment." The office wasn't really a room but a big area with a desk for Miss Claire and a squeaky filing cabinet. The examination room and the treatment room filled one side. Wooden folding chairs lined the office wall. An inside bathroom had been built into a corner with fresh wood—so new it hadn't been painted yet. It had been a while since I smelled new wood. That would have been when Brother Blues built a room on his house for Bailey Renfroe when his granny died. I drew in the scent and held it inside as long as I could to save it for later.

I think now how strange it was that no other girls were there when I went for my shots. I expected girls from school or their mothers. Anybody. I saw nobody but Nurse and Miss Claire. The doctor was nothing but a voice in the other room. Looking back, I wonder why Miss Claire didn't ask how Nurse knew I needed shots and not something else. M'dear must have thought Miss Claire, with all her schooling, would know what was to happen to me.

What I can't forget more than anything was the loneliness. Free Women's Clinic was the most lonesome place ever.

Some things, I don't know. Some things, I do. I once picked up an old burl out of the cow pasture and took it home. It had circles inside circles inside circles. Interesting how a mistake of nature can make something so beautiful. I understand now that's my life. You live in the center of circles, each washing away from the other, like ripples in the cattle pond near the ridge. The movements, you may not see, but even so you feel them. Little ones can soothe, but strong ones can knock you down.

As Miss Claire drove me back home from my first visit to the clinic, I tried to think of something soothing to make my mind off the pain from the shot. I thought of my best friend, Bailey Renfroe.

Chapter 5

Bailey Renfroe and his granny moved outside Hyssop in 1963. We were both seven. They settled in a little house off by itself out past Brother Blues' store. The dirt road leading there stopped at the sugarcane press.

When we was younger, me and him would play spy. That was the best. Some days, we chased each other and threw a ball over the roof till dark called us inside. I won every time. I won because Bailey Renfroe was so round and slow that he huffed and puffed like his granny when she switched Old Mule to move on.

The press hasn't worked since Old Mule kicked Granny Renfroe in the chest when me and Bailey Renfroe was in the fourth grade. He ran out of the house when he heard the thump and fell on his granny wailing, not knowing what to do. After a time, he rose up and went to get Brother Blues. Brother Blues spoke words over the grave the next week, and after the funeral he took Bailey Renfroe home with him. As M'dear and me stood by the open grave, M'dear announced, "She's dead, all right."

Bailey Renfroe came to Hyssop round. So did his granny. Coming down the road, they looked like two cantaloupes walking on sticks. They stayed round as long as I knew them. Bailey Renfroe's hair was buzzed so short that, from a distance, he looked bald. Though they lived in a smaller house than me and M'dear, they had a radio and wooden bed frames. Granny Renfroe had an electric stove in the kitchen and a big refrigerator and a pump organ she played at night. We could have put everything we owned in the back of Mr. Gibbon's pick-up truck: a bed and dresser for me, M'dear's bed and a straight chair, a couch and a little Formica table with four wooden chairs, none of which matched, and my shoe box for Baa.

They didn't have a living room like me and M'dear, but I knew they didn't have to rely on a pouch of money coming every Monday like M'dear did. In the spring, trucks of Mexicans would appear out of nowhere to plant the fields with sugarcane and then disappear. At cutting time, they reappeared and took down the cane. Granny Renfroe did the rest.

Behind the house was a barn where Old Mule stayed when he wasn't walking the press. One morning, me and Bailey Renfroe went to the barn to see what we could see. We were probably eight-years-old. We jumped over hay bales until we had to stop for rest. I lay back on the barn floor and looked under the door. Inside the closed room were wooden boxes stacked against the far wall.

"Let's play spy and see what's in them boxes."

"Naw. That's Granny's syrup. Says I'm to leave it be."

"We won't touch nothing. Come on." I stood up and pulled Bailey Renfroe by his arm until he gave in and shook me free.

The wooden door proved to be heavier than it looked, and it squeaked like an angry squirrel when we pulled it open. I glimpsed around to see if the door was telling on us, but nobody appeared. Old Mule didn't even switch his tail. This room had no stalls, just boxes stacked around three walls. I moved to the closest box and tiptoed to look inside. Pint canning jars, jar after jar, filled the box. I took one out and held it to the sunshine. Clear liquid sloshed inside. "Bailey Renfroe, look at this." I shook the jar. "Sorghum's dark as I recollect it. This ain't dark at all."

"Odom, put that back. You said you wouldn't touch it." Bailey Renfroe always called me Odom. He claimed Margaret Ann was too sissified and took up too much breath to say.

"Ain't hurting it none. Let's taste it. Never tasted no clear sorghum." I twisted the lid and opened the jar. I sniffed. Sorghum smells like scorched sugar, dark, almost tart. It's sticky and thick. What I smelled was light, pure liquid. It was short on the sweetness of sorghum. "Must be some special syrup. Bet she gets a pretty penny for a jar of this." I tipped the jar to my lips. The liquid burned my tongue then my throat as I swallowed. "Yuck. Don't see putting this on a biscuit or in a cake. Here, you try." I handed the jar toward Bailey Renfroe.

"No. Granny says stay out of her jars." He backed away.

"She won't know. We'll seal it back up and nobody'll notice." I held out the jar again. "Come on." I threw out a bribe. "You can sleep in my treehouse."

His eyes opened big. "Promise?"

"Pinky promise." We interlocked our left pinky fingers and jerked them down.

He took a deep swallow. "Whew." He coughed. "That's powerful syrup."

"Let me try again." I reached for the jar. "Give me another swallow."

Bailey Renfroe giggled and handed me the jar. I downed twice what he had drunk and shook my head.

"You ain't besting me, Odom. Give me the jar."

We played besting for a while, until I looked at the jar, now more than half-empty. My stomach burned. My head swam. I had to swallow not to puke. I leaned toward Bailey Renfroe and toppled on my face. He dropped next to me, laughing so hard snot ran out his nose. "Damn, Odom, I think you and me, we're drunk on sorghum."

"We drunk alright, but this stuff ain't no regular sorghum. I think your granny's making some kind of special brew and we done stole half a jar." I rested on my back in the straw.

"How we getting out of this, Odom?" Bailey

Renfroe tried to lift his head but failed.

"I say we put water in the jar and seal it back up. We ease out of here and get in my treehouse like we ain't been nowhere else. Nobody won't know no different. We can say we been at my house all day. M'dear's ironing. She won't notice."

And that's what we set out to do. The one thing I left out was the number of times we stopped along the road and puked in the ditch.

We reached the intersection where my road led through the pasture. There on the store porch sat Brother Blues on the bench. Part of a metal Grape Nehi sign nailed to the wall showed behind him. Bailey Renfroe and me eyed each other. Our looks said we had to be sly else we would be caught in our theft. We lowered our chins and walked on.

As we got closer, Brother Blues called out, "What you two been into?'

We walked on, not answering.

"Come up here where I can see you."

Bailey Renfroe sidled closer to the porch. I took in the whole of the porch. From where I stood, there was Brother Blues and the word "hi" left over from the Nehi sign next to his left arm.

Brother Blues and his massive body and the little word "hi" was the funniest thing I ever did see. I raised my hand and moved it in a broad semi-circle as my response to his "hi." The giggles started and wouldn't stop. Every time I looked at the big man and the little word, I giggled harder. I giggled so hard I barely heard him say "Come up here, Margaret Ann Odom." He sounded as gruff as a bear, not that I ever heard a bear.

By this time, Bailey Renfroe was laughing so hard he was rolling on the porch floor with his legs pulled up to his chest. He laughed so hard he had to wait to catch his breath. Then he stopped.

I staggered up the steps and bent over him. His eyes were shut tight. "You dead, Bailey Renfroe?" He didn't answer. Exhaustion dropped me to my knees, and I nudged his shoulder. He didn't move. If he was dead, I couldn't help it. I put my head on the porch floor and fell asleep in a blink.

Brother Blues woke us at dusk. He called his grown son, Junior, to take us home in the truck and let us out. "No need to tell they got drunk on the granny's rum," he said. "Women'll figure it out."

I never asked Bailey Renfroe what happened

to him, but that night I had the only switching M'dear ever gave me. I wasn't allowed to go back to Bailey Renfroe's house to play. After a long begging time, M'dear agreed he could come visit me, and it was a good thing. Otherwise, I wouldn't have had no schoolbooks after I ran away.

It was after that day I knew how alone I was. With not being allowed to go to Bailey Renfroe's, I was left at home with Hazel. She, being a heifer and all, and me, we grew real close during that time.

Chapter 6

My second trip to the clinic was the same, but different. Three days had passed, and a hard knot had formed on my left hip from the shot. I could feel it when I rubbed my hand back there. Maybe I should have told M'dear, but I didn't want to disappoint her. I knew how much M'dear wanted a good life for me. For her, a good life meant not being sick.

And I knew Nurse could see the swelling. I thought she would give my shot in the other hip, but she didn't. She stuck the needle right into that knot. A deep burn shot down my leg and settled in my foot. I called out and dropped my head on the table. I cried so hard my shoulders shook and my nose ran. I wiped the snot on my skirt. My hip and leg throbbed. I limped out of the room. Nurse never offered a word.

Miss Claire was not at her desk. I went back to the door and raised my hand to knock. We needed to talk about this. I heard Nurse talking to Dr. Graves. I strained to hear. What they said made my stomach turn rock hard.

"The eugenics might not work. She's awfully young," Nurse said.

I struggled to make sense of the strange word. "Blue jennies?" I never heard of blue jennies. How could they know I had blue jennies when they had seen me only twice?

Doctor was talking now. "At least they'll keep her clean. No filthy monthly rags to deal with, but it might require more shots per week."

I gulped hard and refused to let my legs run. More shots? I had had two that first week. A wooden folding chair sat near the side exit, and I lowered myself onto the side of my butt that didn't hurt. Maybe I could ask Miss Claire about the blue jennies, but she wasn't there.

I had to think about something else. A *Good Housekeeping* magazine lay on the chair next to me. I opened to page 37 to read about cakes. I don't know why. M'dear and me had nothing for cooking up fancy cakes.

"Clean," he had said. Me and M'dear always bathed. I breathed a shuttering breath. I should read, but I couldn't read. My eyes were too full of tears. I needed to cry some more, but I worried that if I cried and Miss Claire saw me I couldn't come back. M'dear would be disappointed in me for being a baby.

I slapped the magazine shut. I would wait. No. I would leave. M'dear would understand. She didn't want me to hurt. I limped to the front door and tugged. Locked. Over to the side door. Locked. My breath puffed in and out. Trapped. My hands sweated. I wiped them down my skirt. My jaw clinched. I looked for another door out. There wasn't one. All at once, a shudder ran down my body. Miss Claire had left me locked in with Nurse and her needles and slapping. I licked my lips and gulped. I had no answer. I sat again in the folding chair, pulled up my legs and dropped my head on my knees. Tears wet my skirt.

When my head cleared, I hobbled back to the side door. I looked again at the door we had come in. One door out. One door in. I took a step to try to open the side door out again. Fierce pain shot from my hip to my toes. My knee buckled, and I gripped the doorknob. I had had enough. I was finding an open door, walking out, and not coming back.

Miss Claire stepped out of the bathroom and said, "Ready to go?" I nodded and backed away, hoping she hadn't wondered why I was standing by the door.

I did go back, week after week. I couldn't quit after one week. I meant to be the child M'dear took pride in, as I was her only one.

This time on the way home, my thoughts were full of M'dear and all the pains she took to make sure I would have the best future she could create for me. Making sure I went to school and getting us to church every Sunday. Church ordered our lives. Getting ready started on Saturday night. We had to dress respectable. M'dear put Vaseline on my white patent shoes and ironed my dress. Before we left, she plaited my hair in two braids and set my flat straw hat on my head. I never wanted the green ribbons tied. That made the hat too hot, but M'dear always tied them into a broad bow under my left ear. The hat and me walked down the road with M'dear talking all the way there and all the way back.

We'd walk swinging hands and M'dear would say, "Now you need to know this, Sugar Baby." It seems strange for her to call me that after she'd gone and named me for a town woman she saw in a dentist's office down south in Eufaula. Then she started in gifting me with a memory she thought I needed to know.

M'dear never had a man to walk her down the road for meeting. You'd never know it. Pride stuck out her chin and threw her shoulders back. I wanted all along for Walter Gibbons to walk us down the road. He would've made me a good daddy. I never told her though, because she always said, "You and me, Margaret Ann. We're all us needs." But when I conjure up a father, he would be like Walter Gibbons. He's the White man who worked in Hyssop before he left saying he might be headed for California. He had the prettiest reddish hair and freckles. And a Braves baseball cap that shielded his pale blue eyes. He went to Atlanta in 1967 to see Hank Aaron play and came home with this cap and its fancy "B" on the crown. Part of his job was to look after my daddy's cows.

He brought M'dear money every Monday morning from somewhere and ironing from rich wives in Sweetwater. He'd come by Friday after work and pick up what she'd ironed and bring the week's ironing money with him. Sometimes, I thought he had set up the ironing jobs for M'dear to help us out. She took the money pouch without a comment. For M'dear, if she didn't say it out loud, it wasn't so. And if it wasn't so, there wasn't no shame.

My actual daddy, a White man named Hank Bullard, had given us the house and its garden spot when his mama died.

M'dear met my daddy while working for his mother, Mrs. Bullard. M'dear left school at the age of eleven and began helping her mama work in Mrs. Bullard's kitchen. Three years later, M'dear's mama died in front of Mrs. Bullard's GE refrigerator. After the body was taken away to Eufaula Memorial Funeral Home, Mrs. Bullard called M'dear in from the porch. She had a tin bucket and brush in one hand and a bottle of bleach in the other.

"Here." She held the supplies out to M'dear. "Scrub this floor."

M'dear stood with her back to the refrigerator. "Ma'am? Mama cleaned it this morning before . . ." and she started to bawl.

"Quit that sniveling. Right here." Mrs. Bullard pointed to the floor. "Where you're standing. Right there. Where she lay. It's my kitchen, for God's sake. Use plenty of this bleach." She set the bucket and bleach down and left.

M'dear knelt on her knees and poured straight bleach onto the floor. Either the smell of the bleach or the burden of the day opened her heart and M'dear cried and cried. She finished with hands scalded ashy from the chemicals. What splashed up on her cotton dress ate through the cloth, leaving holes that grew bigger with time.

Before M'dear's mama was cold in the ground, Mrs. Bullard had a carpenter over to box in the end of the back porch. She was looking after M'dear, she said. She was making M'dear into a slave is what I say. Anyway, the room had a door that opened at one end and had a window at the opposite end. A single bed with one quilt, a straight chair, and a hook behind the door where M'dear could hang her three gray maid dresses. Mrs. Bullard had decided that M'dear should start wearing gray dresses topped with white aprons like the other Eufaula maids. M'dear took her holey dress to the edge of the yard and buried it.

M'dear stayed on for four more years, until Mrs. Bullard died rocking on the front veranda. After that, her son Hank Bullard, my daddy, brought M'dear to Hyssop for what he promised would be a better life. Until then, he'd been at college in Tuscaloosa, coming home from time to time. The contacts she'd had with him were those times when she would catch him standing in the kitchen door, staring at her like she was some nickel prize at a fall carnival.

He moved her into our little house in the middle of his cow pastures. I was born not too much later. My own memories of my daddy blend somewhat with M'dear's stories about him. He was seven years older than M'dear and tall. He looked like what I thought a movie star would look like, with his blond hair shaved short against his scalp and standing straight up on top.

Not that my daddy was a bad man, but he got mean-spirited, saying words like "nigger" and accusing M'dear of having bucks sniffing around our house, especially when he'd been drinking. He got so riled up when the government told him coloreds had to be paid the same as Whites, he couldn't get past it. Him saying it and knowing all the while how such words cut into M'dear's feelings. With the re-telling, M'dear could shake her head and shake her head, but there they stayed, them words. He never quit saying it until he left, even with M'dear begging him not to say such in front of me.

M'dear says he had seemed almost happy when he first saw me. He gave M'dear the deed to our house and the acre of land. To keep us safe, she rolled the papers and put them in a gallon jug and buried them in the wide V at the base of my chinaberry tree. But he lost interest in me when his new wife had a boy six years later. If M'dear had had somebody to argue with about what Daddy was like, she would have told you he had just got hard in the heart. "That's the way of it, I reckon." And she said it out loud to make it true.

Me and M'dear had learned never to expect Daddy. If he did show up, we knew it would be after dark. Why, M'dear didn't know. There was nobody about to see him coming or going except Blues Marshall. The fact that he was driving down the dirt road that led to our house didn't say he was doing nothing more than checking on his cattle.

Chapter 7

The day after my second visit to the clinic, M'dear sent me to Brother Blues' store to trade eggs for Lipton tealeaves. I slipped my stuffed black lamb into my dress pocket and set off walking down the road.

Mr. Gibbons, the man who kept my daddy's cattle, had given me the lamb as a present when I was born. M'dear told me about the first time he saw me. He had found her in the porch rocker with me in pink bundling.

He pulled my lamb from behind him and shook it in my face. "What you got there, 'Phelia? A little girlie?"

"Sure is," M'dear answered.

"What you going to call her?" he asked.

"Margaret Ann Odom."

"Mighty fancy name for such a little one." Mr.

Gibbons pulled his finger away and ran it down my cheek.

"It's a proper name. A name any girl can have. Not just a colored name."

Mr. Gibbons nodded.

The lamb had come with a soft covering over its body. Over the years, most of the fur had begun to rub off, leaving it with gray bald spots on its head, back, and belly. M'dear fussed at me for lugging the stiff-legged toy around day after day. She had tried shaming me by telling me I was too old to be cuddling a toy, certainly not a soft-bodied toy like my Baa.

I arrived at Blues' store and opened the screen door to find Nell Hawkins sitting on the nail barrel. Nell's legs splayed so far apart the baby in her belly rested on the barrel's lid. Nell saw me looking at her baby belly.

"You wanting a baby?" she said.

My face burned. I didn't recall ever seeing a girl with her legs spread out so. I also didn't recall ever seeing a baby pooch out like hers. I looked to Brother Blues and set my basket on the counter.

Nell Hawkins had come to Hyssop after Christmas the past school year. I saw little of her with me in the seventh and her in the ninth grade. Having yet another pregnant girl in school didn't surprise me. After the birthing, most girls left them home with their mothers or grandmothers, but Nell brought her little boy to school whenever she wanted. Now here she was, a ninth grader, ready to drop another baby off the wrong side of the blanket.

"You can have this one. I don't need it." I could feel Nell's eyes on my back across the store. "I got a bigger one at home."

"Ignore her. Ain't herself these days," whispered Blues.

My hand trembled as I released the basket handle on the counter. "M'dear needs some Lipton's."

"Margaret Ann? Margaret Ann Odom? You needs this baby," Nell gurgled deep in her throat. I turned to see if she was teasing me. "Got a silly lamb in your pocket. My baby might like that lamb." Nell pointed at Baa and then slammed her fist against her belly.

I gripped Baa. "Stop that. You want to hurt your baby?"

"Leave her be," said Blues. I wasn't sure if he was talking to me or Nell Hawkins.

"You high-hatting me, yeller?" Nell hopped down from the nail barrel. "You better than me? You ought to go on and go to the White school over in Sweetwater."

I tried to ignore her, but a metallic click caused me to spin around. Nell held a long switchblade knife that had popped out of its handle. Her eyes goaded me. "Fight. I dare you."

I backed toward the counter. Brother Blues stepped toward her with both palms open.

"Now, Nell, calm down here. We ain't having no cutting in my store." He moved closer as he talked.

Tears covered Nell's face and she dropped her arm. The knife hung limp. It had lost its need to feed. Brother Blues took the knife and closed the blade. I didn't know that I had held my breath until I breathed again.

As Brother Blues took the knife, Nell came to life again. "Give me back my knife. That's Willie's knife. Army give it to me. Brought it from Nam after he was shot up. It's my knife. Belonged to my big brother and I want it back. I want it back right now." She lurched toward Brother Blues.

"Get it from your daddy. I ain't giving it back to you. You too hot-headed this summer." He put the knife in the bib of his overalls and stepped behind the counter.

Nell turned on me. "You. You, yeller, you done this. I won't forget. You and your long hair flopping about. You thinking you better than me. Well, I got Joey and I'm having a new Willie all for myself. You, you ain't got nothing. You ain't even got no daddy."

My chest drew up tight. I bumped into the counter's edge. I had been moving backwards with every one of her mocks. I couldn't go no further. I clutched Baa tighter. I was stuck.

Patsy, Nell's shadow in crime, opened the screen door. "What's a matter, Nell?"

"Nothing. Let's get out of here 'fore I slice up pretty girl's face."

Patsy stepped outside, and I picked up the basket Brother Blues had emptied. He had replaced the eggs with a box of Lipton's. I loosened my grip on Baa. He was safe. I thanked Brother Blues in a shaky voice.

Brother Blues came around the counter and hugged me. "Don't you worry none, Margaret

Ann. She's jealous, that's all. All talk. Ain't over losing her brother to the war."

Bailey Renfroe appeared through the back door.

"See she gets home, Bailey."

"No thanks, I can make it on my own." I didn't want Bailey Renfroe to see me crying. He'd think I was some kind of baby myself.

Outside, Patsy had waited around the corner of the store. Hearing the screen door shut, she popped out to walk across the road with Nell. I didn't look Patsy's way. Behind me, I heard Patsy tell Nell that she'd take care of this. Not to worry.

On the road home, I talked to Baa. "I don't need no baby. You don't give a baby away. Look at M'dear and how she coped all these years without me having no daddy. M'dear, she never say 'I love you, Margaret Ann,' but she never give me away." I nuzzled Baa with my nose. "Silly M'dear."

Chapter 8

My daddy left us in the fall of 1960 and never came back. I was almost five. Some scientists say people can recall as far back as age three. I believe it because I recall everything. Fact is, I question the power to forget. Things get stuck in my mind and push everything else out. Two straight nights he came, and the events stayed with me.

He jerked M'dear from joy to grief in less than twenty-four hours. He scared me. That first night he took a chair at the kitchen table and propped his hat on his knee. He ran his hand around the brim and waited as I watched him carefully. Sometimes he brought me a Baby Ruth. "For being good for your mama," he said. But not either of those nights.

Cool fall air had caused the chinaberry tree to drop its leaves. It cast moon shadows like bony skeletons through the windows. Daddy spoke to M'dear. "Are you ready?"

M'dear unplugged the cord of her iron and slid the ironing board against the kitchen wall. "I got some eggs I can fry you."

"Eggs? That all you ever eat?" He stepped behind her and put his hands on her hips. Whenever he did that, I knew I'd be going to bed soon.

"Got to eat what I got, I reckon." She turned to find him in her face.

He spoke into her neck. "I'll bring you a side of beef next trip."

"Where would I keep a side of beef? Barely got room for my eggs, butter, and bacon in this little ice box." She pulled away from him and opened the cabinet door. "Got me some grits up here, if they ain't got bugs yet." I heard a deep tired in her voice.

"Forget eating. I came to see you." He twisted M'dear around. I opened my mouth to tell him to stop before he hurt her.

"Let me wash up a bit then. Margaret Ann, get your gown on and go to bed."

She had called me "Margaret Ann," so I knew she meant it. I nodded, but I didn't move.

M'dear closed the bedroom door behind her. When she opened it again, she stood like a princess, her hair fluffed out, her white batiste gown draped over her brown body.

Daddy followed her toward the bedroom, leaving the door open. "I want lights."

"You ain't never before." She saw me standing outside my bedroom door. "Go on to bed now, Sugar Baby."

"Turn on the lights like I told you." Daddy stood between M'dear and the door. He eyed me. "Get into that bedroom, girl," he snapped. "You don't want me to have to make you." He unbuckled his belt.

"Don't scare her like that. She's just a baby," M'dear said.

Daddy whirled to face M'dear. "She's four. Four ain't no baby." He grabbed his felt hat from the floor and threw it on the kitchen table. Fifty-eight years ago, and I still remember the steel cold of his eyes as they cut into me. He ranted as he unbuttoned his shirt. "I brought you here so you wouldn't be sleeping in the street. You telling me what to do now?" He fumbled with his shirt buttons.

"I didn't . . ."

"I own this land. I own Sweetwater. It's my town. I own radio stations and I'm getting into television. I plan to own this whole goddamned state before I quit. Going to be governor next election. You hear that? Governor." He quieted down. "Truth is, I own you, you just don't know it yet." He stumbled as he tried to unthread his belt through the loops. "Shit."

She wiped his spit where it hit her cheek. "Please. Not in front of the baby."

"She ain't no baby no more." He raised his head as he lifted his belt.

M'dear flinched. I could already hear the slap of leather.

"Don't you be questioning me 'bout nothing." He threw his belt across the kitchen.

M'dear refused to move. "I wasn't questioning you."

"Humph," Daddy snorted as he walked to the front door. He left with his shirt open, his belt forgotten. But he had his hat on his head just right.

M'dear caught the screen before it slammed. That night she slept next to me in my bed.

"Don't he like us anymore?" I asked her.

"Shush" was all she said.

The next night as the moon tried to come back, Daddy stomped up on the porch. He opened the door, took a chair at the kitchen table across from me, and propped his hat on his knee again. His head nodded a bit.

"You look tired." M'dear moved to wipe his brow.

He jerked away from her touch. "You wouldn't know. You people don't get tired like us."

She dropped her hand. "Tired don't know no color."

Daddy watched his hand as he ran his fingers around the brim of his hat and sat silent. He took out a cigarette and tapped it on the tabletop.

I expected him to light it, but he only tapped, tapped, tapped, packing it tighter and tighter against the oilcloth. According to M'dear, he had once been skinny, but now his belly hung over his pants.

"Where's my belt?"

M'dear pulled it out of a cabinet drawer and laid it on the table. "Go on. Say it. Been needing to say it some time, I reckon," M'dear said as she faced him. "Say it out loud."

He gripped his hat, picked up his belt, and stood. "I'm not coming back."

"I see," M'dear whispered. She clutched her chest as if his words tried to shove a sharp shriek for survival from her lungs and out through her throat. She clinched her teeth and held it in.

He lifted his brows. "You not going to argue?"

"Don't reckon I got the right," M'dear murmured. She stared at something in the corner. I looked. It was a broke button from my red jumper. "I's your slave. Been so ever since you took me out of your mama's kitchen."

"M'dear?" The tension in the room made me hug myself under my arms.

"No." His eyes darted back and forth. "No, you ain't." He sounded kind of gentle. I relaxed a little.

What he had said the night before about owning her must have stuck with M'dear. She meant to have her say. "Long as there be Whites, coloreds be slaves. Working for Whites'll be endless. Comes from the Bible down to today. No matter what you call it, it still slaving when they ain't no pay."

"Business is business. I'm a business man getting on in politics. You're just politics now." His forehead wrinkled into deep cuts. He straightened his back and patted his back pants pocket. "Me and Mama talked it all out last night."

"You been drinking again." M'dear stepped toward my bedroom. "Go on to bed now, Sugar Baby." When M'dear came near, I smelled a wet dog. It was her fear seeping out. The scent froze me against the wall.

He stepped toward her, his fist clenched. "You and the girl'll be taken care of." He twitched and glared at the window as if he watched something watching him.

Above the window hung upside-down stalks of hyssop tied together with twine, their former green leaves and purple blooms now brown and crinkly. "What's that?" Daddy nodded toward the dead plant. "Some voodoo plant?"

"Last year's hyssop. You seen it. It's always there. Keeps evil out."

Daddy stared at the window. I looked to see what he saw. All I could make out was branches of my chinaberry tree.

"This ain't your house, Mama," he muttered, his chin on his chest. "Get out of here." He jerked his head as if his neck fit too tight. He rocked back and forth in place.

M'dear tilted her head as if he was calling her Mama, but he never had before. He backed away from the window, and we knew. The panic in his eyes showed he saw more than me or M'dear did. My breath came in short spurts so fast I could feel it outside my chest.

"Your mama, she dead." M'dear faced her fear with a deep breath. "These six long years now."

Daddy never blinked.

M'dear had moved across the kitchen, now by the cabinet, as if she had floated there while I wasn't paying attention. She reached behind her back and eased open the knife drawer. The drawer squeaked, old wood against new where Mr. Gibbons had replaced a rotted board.

I held my breath, but Daddy didn't question the sound. My feet had grown to the floor.

"I ain't letting you." He lurched toward the open window.

M'dear grasped a butcher knife and held it behind her. She moved closer toward me. In the dimly lit kitchen, he looked massive. I knew he would get past her if he tried to get to me, but he would leave bloody. His heavy breathing had drowned out the cicadas singing at the cattle pond.

"You know your liquor, Mr. Bullard, turns you crazy." Her body trembled. Her every breath sustained her no more than a thimbleful of air would have. I could see her chest heave. All the severe talking had drawn the air from the room. I should be able to breathe for her. She was my M'dear. She swallowed. I could tell by the way she licked her lips that she needed water to shrink her swollen tongue. I yearned for outside air.

"I ain't claiming no half-breed kid." He slapped his hat on his head and moved toward the door, still talking to somebody M'dear and me never saw. "She ain't your grandchild. I need me some time."

I moved into the light. "Daddy?" I swallowed, trying not to cry, but I did.

"Don't call me Daddy, kid." He spoke without looking at me. "Not to nobody."

M'dear heard the pain in my crying. Behind her, her knuckles turned pale as she clasped her butcher knife. She followed him across the room as he mumbled about leaving all he had worked for to some high-yeller. Without another word, he left. M'dear stayed back. She closed and locked the porch screen and the front door. She hugged the wall until we heard him crank his truck.

"Got some hard, hard demon bearing down on him." M'dear seemed to have forgotten that I was there and spoke to the dark in the room. "What's eating on him will gobble up his soul. That man, he won't survive." Her talking out loud was truth for her but not for me.

Frogs at the cattle pond hushed. Night birds held their breath. Quiet filled the room. Then a screech of metal against metal ruined the stillness. I ran across my bedroom and stepped out the window onto the thick limb of my chinaberry tree where I could see the yard. The porch light showed where Daddy had drove his truck over the inside fence. A space two sections wide lay flat on the ground. Maybe Mr. Gibbons could put it back up before the cattle realized they could come up on our porch.

That was the last time I ever saw my daddy. Mr. Gibbons did come the next morning and re-strung the barbed wire. After that night, Daddy sent Mr. Gibbons with the Monday money.

It was fine he didn't come back. M'dear didn't want me doing something as foolish as Bella Whitstone's girl had when she found out her daddy was the banker over in Roland's Bend. A White man so rich he shit ten-dollar bills, and he never gave Bella one dime for raising his high-yeller. The girl ran off with a barkeep down in Montgomery who promised her the moon and found herself pregnant and stranded outside Atlanta. She came back home, and her mean-spirited step-daddy took her in the side door of the funeral parlor where old man Abrams almost ruined her. No more than fourteen she was.

When we heard the story, M'dear promised, "I got more judgment than a pea-brained bird like Bella Whitstone. I'll see nothing like that happens to you."

Chapter 9

In 1963, Alabama was aflame with what to do about us coloreds wanting a life like everybody else. In Tuscaloosa, the National Guard and the attorney general came down from the capital of the United States to the university. And in Birmingham, that devil Bull Connor brought in a hundred dogs for policemen to release on the colored children, the children who'd been sent out because their mommas and daddies thought they wouldn't be attacked. Used fire hoses to plaster people against walls. The fierce water slid them across the pavement so hard they rose up with scrapes on every exposed part of their bodies; scrapes that grew into scars for everybody to see. Scars bigger than mine.

I saw pictures at school and in Brother Blues' newspaper. I could see those same pictures forming in M'dear's mind from time to time. Her brow would scrunch up and her head would droop and then she'd close her eyes and be very, very still. I thought she was being scared for herself, but she was being scared for me and me having to grow up knowing disregard and violence. "Won't be going to Bombingham," she declared. "No. Not ever."

On Sundays, we went to church. Brother Blues kept M'dear up to date about the goings-on. He's a big-boned man, tall and dark with graying hair. He wears starched overalls and big polished work shoes. Hyssop looks to him for guidance. If Hyssop had a mayor, it would be Brother Blues.

Blues Marshall dressed in a starched white shirt M'dear had ironed. He tucked a handkerchief into his overall's bib to have handy for wiping sweat. M'dear would have ironed that, too.

M'dear relied on his word for her truth. She didn't read, though she knew numbers real good. She got her learning from day-to-day living, and that made her seem older and younger at the same time somehow. We didn't get a television or radio until early in 1974. We had Brother Blues. Brother Blues didn't claim to be schooled in preaching, but he did hold church every Sunday afternoon in the back room of his store in winter and under the oak tree behind the store when it was hot. He started at three o'clock sharp. He mixed his religion and politics as if they were cake batter and it all came out tasting just right. So for M'dear, he had to be an honest man.

"Times a changing," Brother Blues told us one Sunday. "Changing fast. Us coloreds got to be willing to change with the times."

M'dear was ready to change, but she needed to change in her own way. Ask M'dear any day, and she would say straight out that she never wanted a television or radio. In her mind, one honest man's word was better than any stranger's. Strange White people talking out of a box in her living room, acting like they belonged there, unnerved her.

Sundays were for socializing and for religion. M'dear and me got the religion part, but we missed out on the socializing. I'm mulatto, as I said, and it shows.

That Birmingham turmoil wasn't all that was stoking fires around us. Nell Hawkins and Patsy Green lived above Nell's daddy's barbershop with Nell's little boy. Patsy and Nell were always together, and they hugged a lot, even in public. Since the barbershop stood across the road from the store, Nell came to church every Sunday, toting her baby boy who was just past crawling. Not Patsy. Patsy never showed her face at church. That was the only time Nell didn't have Patsy following behind or hanging her arm over Nell's shoulder.

Nell walked out the back door of her daddy's shop and appeared one Sunday at meeting. Nobody knew where she had been or who the baby's daddy might be. She let Joey run in amongst chairs and crawl into the laps of the matrons without saying a word.

Bailey Renfroe was there on Sundays, mainly because he had to live with Brother Blues after Old Mule kicked his granny in the chest and we buried her. Him and me, we were going to seventh grade after that summer.

I would have married Bailey Renfroe. He had been my best friend and playmate, but that summer would be his last. Everybody's life changed when Nell Hawkins showed up. She saw to that. I would have to grow a bit before I figured out that Nell Hawkins wasn't the all of my troubles. At the time, I was convinced she was. I stayed tense as a wire, ready to tear into her once she started to pick on me.

Chapter 10

It was the second week of shots and early August. Samson the bull had gone crazy. I sat on the porch reading a mystery book, when I heard a yelping sound from across the pasture. I ignored it. *Stray dog nipping at some heifer's heels*, I decided. As the sound came closer, I jerked my head up at the sound of hoof beats. Samson. Coming my way.

In front of Samson raced a coffee-colored pup. He was all tail and ears, less than a year old. That ornery bull was chasing it toward the house, head lowered for the kill. The closer Samson came, the huger he got. I jumped up, and the pup ran between the wire fence and the ground. I opened the screen door to let the puppy in. I slammed the screen behind me. Samson knocked the gate down and stopped at the edge of the porch, snorting and pawing. I expected him to climb the steps and storm through the screen. I closed the front door. Just in case.

Dog days and their damp had settled on the land, squeezing out any unnecessary air. The sun dipped closer to the earth by day, boiling tree sap and broiling the leaves. It sat so heavy on Hyssop that at night the ground couldn't recover from the heat. Breathing, especially inside the house, took work.

I found the pup hunkered down under M'dear's chair. Trembling, his tongue dripping from the chase, as he lay on his belly. I crawled toward the dog on my hands and knees. "You okay, little buddy. You okay." The pup backed away without getting up till his tail hit the wall. I reached in, lifted him, and held him close. I took the sheet cover from the couch and wrapped him tight, to stave off his tremors. For two weeks, he slept on my other bed pillow. Every morning before I left for school, I asked M'dear to keep him inside so Samson might forget he was there. But Samson's some kind of elephant. He never forgot.

I didn't name my pup for fear I would lose him to Samson. I figured, if he had no name, I wouldn't miss him. But, name or no, I did miss him. And having no name meant, when I buried him, I had no words to say.

M'dear and me wrapped his smashed body in the old sheet that had been his since the rescue. M'dear helped me dig his little grave by the fenced garden plot. I moved my bed to a different window so I could guard against any night-time varmints tearing into the puppy's grave. And that's how I came to see Hazel in my window.

I was content after a while. I had no need for nobody other than M'dear, Brother Blues, Mr. Gibbons, Bailey Renfroe, of course, and Hazel, my heifer. When I was ten, I found Hazel, new-born, where her mother lay, her blood soaking the ground. Wasn't supposed to be that way, but Mr. Gibbons had missed the prediction of when the heifer would drop her calf. Rather than face the wrath of Hank Bullard over losing a good cow and its calf, Mr. Gibbons let me take the calf home for M'dear to nurse it and keep it growing good.

With M'dear's help, I kept her alive. Hazel was a stout heifer by the time I was twelve. Hazel followed me about the pasture and, when I left the fence gate open, stuck her nose in my bedroom window be it dusk or dawn. From time to time, M'dear shook her head and said, "I never seen no heifer act like a dog before." But that would be Hazel, always near. She watched from the pasture the morning Nell Hawkins picked on me while we waited for the school bus at Brother Blues' store.

Chapter 11

The day of the wreck was brutal. The heat bore down on our heads so hard I felt my scalp burn. Still no rain. Plants, now scorched, took on the sound of flimsy paper. We had walked no farther than from the clinic to the Jeepster when I pressed my hand under my right arm to soothe the swollen knot growing there. I had begun to receive needle jabs in my arms as well. My dress was wet with sweat. It stuck to my back. Damp hair lay against my neck. I reached up and lifted it to my crown and twisted it into a bun. It fell back against my neck as soon as I released it. It hit heavy.

I didn't start out to cause Miss Claire a problem. I just wanted to go home. It was Friday. I hated the clinic and Nurse and the doctor who talked about me behind closed doors. I wanted to be back in a time when M'dear and me had never met Miss Claire. The ground burned my feet through my shoe soles. I needed a drink of water.

I had been coming at least once a week or sometimes twice for shots against the blue jennies for four weeks now, and I had never seen any other patient at the clinic. I told myself that my appointment must be after the clinic closed to the public. Maybe that was how clinics worked. I knew that I didn't want to come back. If I had blue jennies, I was getting worse, not better. And I did have blue jennies. Dr. Graves and Nurse had both agreed.

These thoughts troubled me as we rode past Brother Blues' store. Bailey Renfroe wasn't on the porch for me to wave to him. The troubles stayed with me as we rode between the pasture fences.

Telling about the clinic trips is like baking a cake. It all gets mixed up, panic mixed in all together with tremors and headaches and not being able to sit straight. You heat the oven, only to see the batter rise and fall into a gummy center. I beat myself up, dreaded the trips in advance. Not that I dreaded seeing Miss Claire. I dreaded Nurse and the pain. Each time it was stronger than before.

So much happened to my body while I went to the clinic. More than I expected. M'dear had told me about my nature coming down when I asked about the rags she bleached and hung to dry on my chinaberry's low limbs.

"A beautiful time, it is," she claimed. "A time for you to have babies of your own to love." All the strange things made me think I might be having my monthlies, but having the monthlies couldn't be as bad as I felt. In fact, I had had no real monthly curse. Not enough to wear a rag. But M'dear believed I would get there. She asked me all spring about spots of blood and about how my breasts felt. I never had a changing answer for her.

I was sick. I hurt like I never hurt before. Drained, as if life had left my body. Nobody recognized what was happening to me. That afternoon, Nurse had seen a spot or two of first blood when I lowered my panties for the shot. It would be my first and my last, but I didn't know that. She shook her head. She always shook her head when I was around.

As a result of several weeks of clinic visits, I had pones on both hips and upper arms from earlier shots. Pockets of pus had formed on each one. Part of me wanted M'dear to notice, but I didn't show her. I had made it a point not to let M'dear see any of these, though she did question me about why I flinched when I tried to lift my arms. I didn't want her to think I had failed her. I could take the pain, if it made her proud. Pain can eat you out. It's a silent cancer gnawing away until there's nothing but bone and skin. No blood left to spark another life.

I was tired, so tired from not sleeping good and from hurting. I'd catch myself asleep before I hit the bed. And when I hit the bed, I'd wake myself with the hurting all over again. Then I'd be awake not knowing which way to turn.

It was a day same as the other days: Nurse, the shot, waiting for Miss Claire. All the same, but I was different. I couldn't say how, but I felt it all over. After the shot, I limped to Miss Claire's desk to find paper so I could concentrate on doing my homework. No paper. I stepped back to rethink what I would do, when there on the floor outside the Treatment Room lay a blank page. *Maybe that ghost dropped it for me*, I told myself and wondered if I should be afraid. I took the paper and began converting teaspoons and tablespoons to cups. My pencil trembled from the jitters. This shakiness was a new thing. To hide it, I clinched my fists and held them in my lap. From inside the Treatment Room, I heard Dr. Graves talking to Nurse about me and the blue jennies.

With my head down, I didn't see the door open. I jumped when Miss Claire came out of the room marked "Ladies."

"Ready to go?"

I folded the paper and slid it into my book. I replaced the large rubber band around the cover to hold the pages in. "Yes, ma'am."

Heat as intense as an in-your-face fire hit us as we walked toward the Jeepster. I stumbled against the pain in my left leg. I grabbed Miss Claire's arm for balance and dropped my book.

"You okay?" Miss Claire asked. "What's got you limping?"

I nodded but didn't answer. M'dear didn't know about the hard lumps. Miss Claire might tell her. I didn't need that. Miss Claire took the book so I could hold her arm with both hands. The book was one of the best we had in our cooking class. Teacher had loaned it to me because I was quiet, a good student. Loose pages stuck from under the covers. A thick rubber band cut through dry paper.

Miss Claire removed the rubber band to straighten the pages. She opened the book and gave me a quick look. "Margaret Ann, where did you get this book? It belongs at the White school."

"I know what you're thinking. I didn't steal it." I snatched back my book. "All our school books are hand-me-downs." I couldn't look at her. "Don't matter none. Words stay the same."

"Not necessarily," she argued.

"It's what I got, so it's got to do." I stuffed the loose pages inside the cover and popped the rubber band back in place. "I don't steal."

Miss Claire slipped her arm around me and squeezed my upper arm. I winced against the pain. Her eyebrows raised in a moment of concern, but she didn't ask.

"That's not what I thought at all." She helped me climb into the Jeepster. "Let's get you home. You look all washed out." She walked around the Jeepster, lowering the back windows and the backdoor glass so moving air might help cool the inside. She cranked the engine and headed toward home.

The empty sky had pushed what clouds there were far into space, offering nothing to cut the heat. I felt limp. I needed a strong wind behind me to push me forward, clearing a path away from the clinic. Something to give me strength. Clouds appeared, dark in the distance, and I laughed to myself at the thought of a magnificent storm rolling over Hyssop. I love storms. I'd missed them. A need to cry came over me when I thought of rain cooling my face and wind lulling my chinaberry. I would stick out my tongue to catch raindrops and they would run down my chin. There had been fog once, moist, silent fog, but not in a long, long time.

Another Friday. Another shot. The closer we got to Hyssop, the harder I clinched my hands. As Miss Claire rounded the last bend and headed down the straightaway that led by the pasture fence, a rash of sweat broke out on my forehead. I made up my mind. After the question of whose book I had, after not seeing another living person in the place to get shots, not ever, after not being able to get out locked doors, I had reason enough. Forget the cool air conditioning. Forget blue jennies. I'd had my last shot today. I stiffened my body and braced my hands against the dashboard. Heat burned my hands. I grabbed the bench seat. We needed to stop.

"Stop the Jeep." I spoke hardly above a whisper.

"Why?" Miss Claire eyed me sideways. We were at least half a mile from my house.

"Stop, Miss Claire." I spoke through tight lips.

She didn't. I grabbed the steering wheel with both hands and jerked it right as hard as I could. The front end of the Jeepster leaned as a sharp drop blew the front passenger tire. The explosion sounded, for all I knew, like a shotgun blast. Miss Claire's forehead slammed into the rearview mirror. I screamed and ducked under the dash. I tried to cram myself into the motor. It was so dark under the dash, I couldn't see nothing. Time slowed down as the Jeep slid, forever it seemed. All I heard were my screams. The Jeepster settled easy in the gully, resting on its passenger side.

"Hush now."

"I wrecked your car!" I wailed. My body shook. I knocked my head against the bottom of the dashboard again.

Strapped in by the waist seatbelt, Miss Claire hung sideways. She reached over and tried to pull me out of my hole. "Get up here. You didn't wreck the Jeep. The Jeep ran off the shoulder. The front tire blew. We slid into the gully." She tugged at my blouse. "That's all we need to say. Now. Get out from under there so we can get out." Miss Claire unbuckled her seatbelt. Without the belt holding her in place, she tumbled over on my body huddled on the floorboard.

My terror yowled. I thrashed my arms around like some panicked bird, trying to push Miss Claire away.

"Shut up!" She shouted into my face.

I fell limp against the door and cried.

"You're okay. Hush." Miss Claire took a deep breath. "We've got to get out. Might be a fire." Bracing against the top, she lifted herself off me. She grasped the steering wheel to hold herself steady. She bumped her body against the driver's door, like she thought her weight would set the Jeep back on the road. It wouldn't move.

"Stop that crying. You need to crawl over the seat and climb out the back window. I'll see if I can get out my window."

"You go out the back." I whimpered. I liked my plan better.

"I'm too big. You'll fit better."

I couldn't argue with that. I shimmied out the back window. Miss Claire appeared. I pulled and she pushed. We both got her out. Somebody passing by would have thought we'd been caught in a rainstorm, we was so wet.

Outside the Jeep, we sat on the bank, two mismatched twins. Both exhausted, our arms hung loose between our knees. Miss Claire sniggered. I followed. You know how you have to laugh when you're so tired and so scared you can't do nothing else. Within a minute, our silly laughter crossed the road and disappeared down the pasture. A deep tiredness took over my body and mind.

"What was that about?" Miss Claire asked as she wiped laughter-tears on her jacket sleeve.

"What?" I eyed the road as if I expected the Savior to walk up, his white robe crimped high in his hands to avoid the dirt.

"You know what. Grabbing the steering wheel like that."

I was caught. I had to tell her. "I'm not going back." I moaned. "I don't want you to come get me anymore," I whispered. My face was flushed, not only from the heat, but also from the shame of having to admit that I quit, that I would be upsetting M'dear .

"Why not? What caused you to want to wreck us?"

My hands trembled. Miss Claire pulled me close. I felt safe, as safe as I had been with M'dear. Miss Claire held me until I calmed down.

"What happened today?" Miss Claire whispered.

"Promise you won't tell M'dear?" I could barely speak.

Miss Claire nodded and looped her pinky finger through mine. She waited.

I hung my head. "I got in a fight today."

"You? In a fight?" She chuckled. "That doesn't sound like you."

I lifted my head and stared at nothing down the road.

"Why did you get in a fight?"

I sniffled. I needed to blow my nose, but I didn't have a handkerchief. "That old nappy-headed girl in my cooking class Nell Hawkins came up behind me and she say 'Your hair so pretty. Can I touch it?'

Before I could say anything, she grabbed a fistful and yanked me down on the floor. I dropped my book and the pages all fell out. I landed on my hip. I teared up cause it hurt so bad. Now everybody's laughing at me sitting in the floor bawling like a baby."

Miss Claire rubbed my back. "Couldn't you get up?"

"They was closing in, and Bailey Renfroe, he was going out to auto mechanics building, and he started picking up the parts of my book, and Nell Hawkins, she say 'High-yeller, you got a feller,' and I says 'No feller want you.' And she kicked me in my sore hip."

"Where were your teachers?"

"Ain't but one other down the cooking hall. Miss Garner. She took me in her room and give me a big rubber band to hold my book together."

"Nell Hawkins?"

"She stroll on off like she own the place. Her and her buddies."

"Well, she don't." Miss Claire patted my hand. "Own the place, I mean. Come on. Let's go get us some help."

"You still okay by me? Even if peoples poke fun?"

"Margaret Ann Odom." Miss Claire turned me toward her and clasped both palms against my face. "If I ever have a little girl, I hope she's just like you." Miss Claire brushed a soft touch across my face. She cupped her hands and collected my tears in her palms. She closed her fingers, holding the tears tight. "Come now." She said. "We'll find help."

Relief filled me up. She hadn't asked why my hip hurt so. I don't know if I could've told her anyways.

Miss Claire placed her forearms in my armpits and lifted me as if I was a toddler rising from a warm water bath. She pulled me to her bosom and fell backwards. She landed on the ditch side, me in her lap. I could smell the scent of fresh shampoo on Miss Claire's hair. She settled and sang a bit of lullaby. "*Hush little baby, don't say a word.*" She dropped into a hum, cradling me. I quieted. I laid my forehead against Miss Claire's and didn't speak.

"Today's Friday. You've got a whole weekend to think it out." Miss Claire stood and stepped into the bottom of the gulley. Her high-heeled pumps sank into soft dirt. She tugged them off and raised her straight skirt.

I could not believe that this grown woman was taking off her clothes on the side of the road. A White woman at that. I whirled away and faced the Jeep.

Miss Claire laughed. "Just taking off these stinging stockings." She reached into the back window of the Jeep and took out a pair of shiny yellow flat sandals. "I don't know why people think wearing stockings and high heels make a person look like she knows what she's doing," she mumbled. After tossing her heels, hose and garter belt into the Jeep, she offered her hand to me. "Let's go," she said. "It's hot as Hades out here." We pulled each other up the bank onto the road.

"Where?"

"Didn't we pass a store back a ways?"

"Blues Marshall's."

"Now, tell me why your hip's sore."

I shook my head. I couldn't tell her I was a coward.

Rather than go ahead and settle in the west, the sun decided to bear down harder on us than before as we walked back the way we had come. The only thing that moved along the road was Miss Claire and me and the dust we stirred up.

Chapter 12

In the distance, we saw Brother Blues at the store. He sat down on the store porch's edge and leaned his back against a two-by-four holding up the tin roof. He waited. It was near closing time, but I wished a strong wish that he would wait us out. Something must have told him to rethink closing, told him "Better wait."

I could tell from when he stood that he had seen us. He had his hand cupped over his eyes. Here we were, two people coming toward the store, one in a tan skirt dragging a jacket and one, clearly me, carrying a schoolbook.

I must have walked like an old woman, hips throbbing, shuffling along behind the White woman. My head hung heavy. I continued to fail M'dear. My shoulders slumped, and I could hear M'dear say "Stand up straight, Sugar Baby. Walk tall." My hands felt so heavy. They pulled my upper arms down, stretching out the tight skin under my sleeves. Brother Blues would tell me later that as I came closer, he could see how peaked I was, how dark circles shadowed my eyes, and my lips were cracking dry. I admit I was miserable.

"What you doing here, Margaret Ann? You don't look too pert." Brother Blues took my elbow and helped me up the step. "You, too," he spoke without any reference to who "you" might be.

I sat on the plank bench that flushed the front wall. A rusty RC Cola sign over my head and my white middy with its red tie were the only colors against the gray boards. That and the Grape Nehi sign. I recalled the day Bailey Renfroe and me laughed ourselves silly. The sign didn't look all that funny this time.

"You ailing, girl?"

I might as well say it out loud. Keeping quiet wasn't making them go away. "I got the blue jennies, I reckon." I dropped my head back and listened to my voice ricochet off the tin roof.

"The what?" Miss Claire frowned. She can make a monster frown.

"Blue jennies. That's what Doc Graves say." My voice sounded drained. I needed a Grape Nehi real bad. "Guess he's right, him being a doctor and all."

Miss Claire's eyebrows shot up. She gave Brother Blues the eyeball. He shook his head. They must have thought I was crazy. First wrecking the Jeep and now claiming to have some never-heard-of disease.

Miss Claire bent closer and whispered. "You didn't tell me this before the wreck."

"You said it wasn't a wreck," I whispered back. I swallowed tears. I didn't need to cry in front of my own pastor.

"Before the tire blew out," Miss Claire amended, raising her voice. She looked at Blues for a reaction but got none. "That's what I meant."

Brother Blues ignored her. "What's your ailments, girl?"

"Sores. On my arms and hips from where she give me shots. And big old hard lumps. I guess they the jennies." I followed a ladybug with the toe of my shoe as it dragged itself across a board. Here was this little, round bug meandering along, minding his own business, while my whole world was falling apart. How I wished I could trade places with that bug.

"Show me your arm," Miss Claire said real gentle.

I turned my back to Brother Blues and pulled the collar of my middy down over my shoulder. Pus blisters covered my upper arm. Purple circles surrounded knots the size of walnuts. Older rings favored the color of rotting green apples. Within each knot was a tiny black prick where the needle had opened the skin.

Miss Claire breathed in deep. "Why's the doctor giving you so many shots?"

"Do Ophelia know you got them jennies?" Brother Blues asked, hard-faced.

"No," I said. Then I reconsidered. "I don't know. I get a shot or two every time I go, and today, Nurse say the blue jennies ain't working so they got to give me bigger shots or I got to come back more days a week." My eyes filled. "I already go twice a week." I looked up at Miss Claire. "I ain't going back, Miss Claire. I hurt all over and I don't want no more." Tears dripped off my chin.

"Too hot out here for you feeling bad. You go inside and get you a Grape Nehi. On me." Brother Blues knows my soul, for sure. He helped me up and turned me toward the door. "Me and this here lady, we got some talking to do."

I hauled myself up and into the store.

"And get you a Baby Ruth while you at it," Blues called over his shoulder. I looked back out the door. He nodded to Miss Claire. "You come over here and sit, missus."

I opened my drink and took a deep gulp. I edged to the open door and sat on the floor. Bailey Renfroe would be proud of me being a spy and all. There, I could watch and hear what he would tell Miss Claire. I hoped he'd say that I couldn't go back. He's my preacher. It's his job to look after me.

"It looks to me like she's not tolerating injections well."

"What injections you talking about?"

"I don't know."

Brother Blues raised his voice. "You telling me you take a child that ain't yours out and give her to some doctor who does what you don't know about to her?"

I felt Miss Claire draw back. "I'm just doing my job here."

"Humph." Brother Blues slipped inside and almost stepped on me, sitting there on the floor. "Get up," he said. "This is grown-up business."

"But it's me, Brother Blues. Margaret Ann. It's about me."

Brother Blues rolled his head around on his neck and walked behind the counter where he sat on his high stool.

Miss Claire called me to come outside. She had picked up my book. She must have thumbed through the loose pages. A half-sheet of paper had fallen to the floor. One side read "Free Women's Health Clinic." Under the heading, someone had penciled in conversions from cups to pint, from pints to quart. My homework. Miss Claire turned the paper over and read "'Order serum supply Monday.' What's this?"

"My homework." I reached for the paper. "Found it on the floor. I thought it would be alright."

"I need it." She folded the paper and slipped it in her purse. I didn't have the energy to protest.

Blues Marshall stepped out next to her and stood straight as a tree. "Come on out the heat."

Inside, he motioned for her to sit in a straight-back chair. "Come on, Margaret Ann."

"Your store, it smells like old motor oil," Miss Claire said.

He spoke without looking at Miss Claire, like he did when he was channeling the Word of the Lord. "The good Lord, he didn't make all animals equal, Miss Whitehurst."

Miss Claire cringed as if stung. She later told me that Blues Marshall was the biggest man she had ever seen. She was right about that. He held no fat, but he stood tall and thick as an ancient oak trunk. His gray stubble made her think of Uncle Remus and Brer Rabbit stories. M'dear had starched his bib overalls and ironed a sharp crease down each leg. His Purexed white dress shirt held marks where he bent his arms against the stiffness of fresh laundered cotton.

"Call me 'Claire,' Mr. Marshall." She put out her hand.

"You can call me Mr. Marshall," and walked away.

Brother Blues lowered his large body onto an overturned keg, and she drew back her hand and clasped it with the other.

Brother Blues heaved himself into a mound and sighed. "You take old Brother Chicken Snake. Now he's going to do what he was made to do."

I slumped against the coolness of the metal chest that housed the colas and waited for his lesson.

Miss Claire sighted Brother Blues' brogan shoes. I followed her eyes. Spit polished and dustless, even on a day with no rain. Brother Blues' brogans always looked better than my Vaselined shoes.

He continued, "Snake's job's to steal eggs out my chicken coop. He finds a hole and lets his long self in without even a knock. Sometimes he winds his black person around the nest and swallows them eggs one at a time. Might rest while he's a waiting for his natural juices to soften the shells. And he might even sleep a bit. But sometimes if something he don't like come along, he just drop off the nest ledge and crack them eggs where he hits the ground. That's a chicken snake for you."

Miss Claire nodded, as if she understood his point. She wiped sweat from her temple and flipped her damp hair off her neck. I flipped my hair too. Tomorrow I would ask M'dear for a braid.

Brother Blues scooched back and rested his back against the counter's edge. "Some hot summer day, you might find Brother Snake crawling slow across the road out there with a hump here and a hump there." He motioned toward the road. "Leaving them eggs whole until he finds a pine tree he can wrap his longness around and crush them eggs. Pop! Pop! Pop!" Blues slapped his thigh with each pop. Miss Claire jumped. "That's what he do."

Brother Blues pulled a wooden matchstick out of his overall bib and bit off the match head. I thought the story was over and moved to get up off the floor. Instead, he spit out the head and nudged it into a wide crack in the floor. Its red tip intact, it disappeared. I imagined a mat of unlit match heads under the store, waiting for an excuse to blaze up. Brother Blues stuck the wooden end between his purple lips and continued. "That's what any Chicken Snake Brother would do."

Miss Claire waited. Her face said she saw no point to his story. The silence was so strong

I heard ice melting and dripping in the drink box behind my back. I followed her eyes as she looked at the shelves to her right. Three cans of Arm & Hammer baking soda. Six of bags sugar. Five loaves of Merita white bread. When Brother Blues spoke, his voice startled us both.

"But you take this fine coon hound dog I had a while back. Best I ever had. Sired by Gold Runner who took the State ribbon in '52. Beautifulest dog you ever seen, he was. Black and tan, coat slick as oil. In no time flat, my neighbor Erskine come knocking on my door down at the house and telling me his eggs was disappearing and his chicks too. I asked him how come. He say it was how come 'cause my fine hound dog was eating them. That's how come." He moved the matchstick to the other side of his mouth with his tongue. "So I says, 'How you know it's my dog?' 'I seen him' he says. So I sets about to catch him. He's my dog, after all. That very night, I took me a sack of flour off the shelf and dusted it all around Erskine's chicken coop. Next morning, paw prints was all about and chicken feathers laid out like speck-led beans. Shore 'nuff. Back home, that fine dog was there sleeping under my oak. Had the whitest feets you ever did see."

"What'd you do?" Miss Claire asked.

"Shot him."

Miss Claire gasped. My head popped up. I never imagined Brother Blues with a gun, but it must be so. Brother Blues said it his own self.

Brother Blues sauntered out and across the porch. We found him leaning against the post, staring down the road toward our place.

"I'll get my boy Junior up here and have him take the girl home to her mama." He spoke without turning. "I reckon you can get on down the road to town and ask that Walter Gibbons to come get Hank Bullard's fine jeep out the gully."

Within the whisper of a breath, Miss Claire disappeared around the bend.

Chapter 13

"Margaret Ann! Margaret Ann Odom!" M'dear called. "You get your own prissy self out here right now!" Heat lightning outlined the hills across the pasture to announce the coming night. A false promise of rain, for the sky never opened.

"Why you yelling at me, M'dear ?" After the wreck that afternoon, I had no energy left.

"Blues Marshall just called here." She looked at me from under her brows. Time for me to edge away. "Says you got something. Something called the 'blue jennies.'" M'dear cocked both hands on her hips as if to say I was making up some fancy tale.

I cut my eyes to the floor so as not to see her disappointed. "Yes, ma'am. I reckon so."

"Look at me, girl." M'dear lifted my chin and

stared at my face. "I never heard tell of no blue jennies. And Brother Marshall, he ain't neither. How do you go about explaining something we ain't never heard tell of?"

"I'm just saying what Nurse say to Dr. Graves."

"And what was that?"

"Say I got to come back more times a week or get stronger shots for my blue jennies. Shots ain't working now." Tears formed in my eyes, but I blinked them away.

"How do she know you got these blue jennies?"

"She didn't like it that I got a spot of my monthly on my underpants today. And lumps and red places around the shots on my arms and my butt, I guess." The tears escape. I put my face into my hands. "I don't want to hurt you none, M'dear, but I don't want no more shots. I told Miss Claire not to come get me. Not ever again. I can't keep hurting and hurting." I sat on the floor then rose again. My butt hurt too much to sit.

"Come on. Get inside. Let's wash that face." M'dear lifted me by my arm but released it when I whimpered. "Go on. Let's see what's this all about." She led me to the kitchen table. We both sat under the hanging bulb.

"Pull off that middy," M'dear said. "We get to the monthlies later."

I had to grunt as I eased the blouse over my head. My arms had gotten that stiff. I showed my upper arms. There was no change from when Miss Claire saw the sores earlier. Where each needle had punctured the skin, there was a circle of pus. Around that was red skin, all sitting atop its hard core.

M'dear laid her open hand on my swollen arms. "You got the fever." She lifted my face to the light. "Your face looks like you been dusted with flour. I'm calling Brother Blues. We going to see what he stocks to clean this mess up. Maybe ride us to the colored doctor past Prattville."

I pulled away. "No. I don't want nobody else to see."

"No matter what you wanting. You going. Put your middy back on. No. Put on a blouse that won't be needing to come over your head so's you can get it off easy." She walked to the phone, all the while talking. "What Miss Whitehurst say 'bout this? She see it?"

"She seen it, but she ain't said nothing to me."

116

I walked toward my bedroom for another blouse. "Reckon she thinks it's all right, her being a clinic worker and all."

M'dear took the phone receiver off its cradle and told Operator to dial Brother Blues at home.

"It's them dog days making them so bad, I reckon, Brother Blues." M'dear said. She held the receiver away from her ear, as if Blues Marshall himself might get too close to her face. "Got a place on her jaw festering up.

No. I ain't tried nothing . . . I can try that. I got Irish potatoes in the bin." She waited for Brother Blues to respond. "And I got powdered sulfur for her jaw. If that don't work, she won't be going to school next week. She got the fever . . . No. She say she ain't going back to the clinic. Can't blame her much myself."

I shifted to my other hip. The shift didn't help. Both sides felt like a summer spider's deep bites had worked themselves into boils. I buttoned the front of a white shirt and tried to find an easy way to place my own self in the chair.

"Well, I thank you mightily. Ain't got no mama to ask myself, but I'll try to get her up and going by Monday. Probably not be at preaching tomorrow, but the Lord, He'll understand . . . A blessed evening to you, too."

Outside, the chinaberry tree swayed in a rising wind, as if it were trying to entice a drop of rain. Sweat ran down my temples and wet my hair.

M'dear hung up the phone and took a sharp knife from the drawer. She put a match to the tip and lifted my arm. I laid my head on the table, too exhausted to protest anymore. It took only a second for M'dear to puncture each sore. I squirmed to get my arm back, but M'dear held firm until she had opened sores on each arm and on my butt. She wiped each opening with a rag soaked in kerosene to kill the poison once it wept out. By the time she finished, I smelled nasty.

M'dear took a firm potato from the wooden bin across the kitchen. After peeling the potato, she scraped the potato using a spoon until she had three tablespoons of moist, soft pulp. She packed the pulp on each open sore and wrapped my arms with strips of clean cloth.

I whimpered at first, but then as the potato moisture seeped into my arm, I screamed. "Take it off!" I cried. "I rather have blue jennies." Lightning lit the room, and I ducked my head.

"Got to be. To siphon out the poison." M'dear scraped more potato and plastered the pulp on my other arm.

I wept. "Please don't do no more," I begged. The shots had not hurt this bad.

"Just these places on your butt and we through. Come light tomorrow, this fever ought to be gone."

Thunder sounded from the direction of Prattville. Within minutes, the storm bypassed Hyssop and dumped its rain closer to Montgomery.

Hampered by house darkness and rag bandages, I let M'dear lead me to bed. As soon as M'dear stepped out of my bedroom, I slipped off the bed and stood, bracing my weight against the bed's foot. Distant rain and the breeze brought in the aroma of wet earth mixed with cow manure. I thought of promises of new life and Hazel's first calf, ready to be born. Wind rose and swatted the house in swells. I stood by the window as coolness wrapped itself around me, and I relaxed. Fresh air told me somebody somewhere had a good dose of hail.

In fewer than five minutes, the air grew still. I got back in bed, sweating against the loss of moving air. I squirmed. If I lay on either side, my upper arms throbbed. If I lay on my left side, my hip added to the pain. Laying on my stomach smothered me. So I stood and again leaned against the iron bed's foot, trying to rest, waiting for sleep to come. Tears came before sleep. I gave in when my left leg began to cramp and tried again to find a comfortable way to lie.

Maybe I should ask M'dear for a St. Joseph's, but she would know that I hurt. And M'dear wanted so bad for me to keep going to the clinic. She hadn't told me so, but I saw it in her face. I would stand the pain. I lifted my body, piece by piece, back on the bed. What sleep I was able to have came only when I lay still as a stump.

Chapter 14

Something in the quiet of the pre-dawn night woke me. I rolled off my stomach and cringed. In the distance but coming nearer, Hazel trotted, bawling with each hoof beat.

Now that I had moved, my breath came easier. I sat up. A dark shadow marked my window. Unsure that I saw eyes, I blinked. There they were. Eyes black as coal, and a nose that reminded me of M'dear's Sunday pocketbook, a dull, black, leathery rectangle with its handle missing.

I moved closer. It was Hazel. All week, I had watched Hazel prepare to birth her first calf. She kept herself away from the herd for the past two days. She should be in the barn or out in open pasture by now, waiting to drop the calf. If she had already dropped the calf, she should be with the calf, not here at my window.

I pushed out the screen and patted Hazel's thick-boned head. "What you doing here?" Hazel bawled, more a moan than an answer. "Time for your baby?" I scratched Hazel's ear. Hazel shook her head and moved away. "Can't help you none, girl." I stuck out my arm. "Look at me all bandaged up."

Hazel moaned again. I opened the window wider and propped it up with a wooden stick. "What you want, little mama?" I whispered. Hazel's mournful bellow scared me. I knew Hazel's talk. She had told me when she was sick, when she was cold or being nosy. "Shush. Be quiet."

Hazel shook her heavy head from side to side and made the most distressful cry. Hazel was scared. She moved away.

"Got to get my shoes." With shoes in hand, I climbed out the window backwards. As I dropped to the ground, my foot hit the stick that held the window open, and the window dropped with a thud. Inside, the clock bonged five times. If M'dear had heard the window, maybe she would think it was six o'clock. She had been on her feet all day, so she might sleep a sound sleep.

Hazel walked the pebble road toward the fence, as if it was one of her familiar paths across the fields. I hopped along, slipping on my Keds. I had pampered Hazel since she was a calf, but I didn't expect the heifer to want me at the dropping. In the moonlight, I couldn't see if Hazel's belly was flat or not. "Leave her be," M'dear often told me. "Heifers ain't dogs." But I knew Hazel. Hazel's different.

With the moon lower on the horizon, the night darkened. I looked back the way I had come. Our little house with its chinaberry tree was no more than a dark shadow. Before me, the dead-end road was too far away to see, so I followed the *clomp clomp* of Hazel's hooves as they hit the gravel.

Realizing how far I had come from the house, I scanned the pasture. Samson could be anywhere. He mostly spent the night in the barn, but I hadn't seen him go in last night. If me or Hazel passed his line of vision, he might charge. Even without a sore hip and arms, I would never have been able to outrun him. I quickened my step so I would be closer to Hazel. She needed me right now.

Hazel picked up speed as she neared the fence. She trotted up to the ungated gap in the fence and stopped at the cattleguard. I know enough

about Angus to know that they step with care,
unlike horses who might put their hoof down an
armadillo hole without a thought. For Hazel to go
to the cattleguard confused me. She knew her leg
could slip between the metal pipes. It could be
broken, or her weight could break her ribs when
she fell. It's nature's way, the wonder of the herd,
how they come to know where not to go.

I caught up with Hazel at the fence opening.
There on the cattleguard lay Hazel's calf, resting
on its belly. The mother in Hazel had known it
needed help. Somehow, it had gotten its front leg
hung through the space between two pipes. This
was bad. Really bad. Newborn, it had to feed, or
it would die.

I bent over and rubbed my hand over the calf's
back. Its coat was dry. It had been born at early
dusk or later. Its bones nudged through its skin.
It was puny. I put my hands under its belly and
tried to lift. The calf bleated and began to bawl.
It thrashed its free legs about, kicking my gut. I
eased the calf down and started back for a flashlight.

Hazel stepped in front of me and nudged
me toward the calf. I went back to the calf, now

bawling ever so soft. I bent my legs and lifted the calf again. It was too light. It should have weighted at least twenty pounds more. When I lifted it, the right leg slid from between the grids and dangled. It was cut and cut bad. Halfway down the leg, clotted blood broke free and ran into my hand.

I forgot Samson and screamed for M'dear. A light appeared in the front window, followed by the front porch light. "M'dear!" I called. "I need you! At the road!"

M'dear ran, her flashlight beam shifting right and left. She stopped before me and the calf. Hazel stood back. M'dear directed the light over me. "What on God's green earth you doing, child?"

"Hazel's calf, it cut its leg." I held the calf tighter. "Real bad." One hand supported the damaged leg. "We got to fix it."

M'dear shined the light on the cut. "Put that calf on the ground. I'll get the axe." M'dear spoke between gasps. "Got to put it down. Cut's too bad. That's what we got to do."

"No," I cried. Tears covered my face. "You can't do that. It's just a baby," I begged. "It ain't done nobody no harm." Hazel nuzzled my back.

"It ain't doing no good neither. Not with no cut-up leg." M'dear reached for the calf. I turned so my mother could not touch it.

"What's Mr. Bullard going to say, us taking in a crippled calf?"

"I don't care what he says. He don't own me. If he don't want it, it can be mine. Mines and Hazel's." I stepped closer to Hazel. "Brother Blues'll fix it. I'm putting it in my bed and going to get him right now."

"No, you won't." M'dear moved to take the calf. "Sunday's hard enough. You ain't going to worsen his Sunday morning."

I backed into Hazel's hard body. "This is my calf and I'm keeping her and her name's Ruby and she's staying with me." I caught my breath. "She needs me to help her. So," I stomped my foot. "Yes, I am."

"You got to stop taking in strays. First that yapping pup and now a no-good calf. Act like a lady." M'dear rubbed her hand across her forehead. "You ought to be growing into your womanhood any day now. I might ought to go to that clinic and ask that doctor about why you ain't having no real monthlies. Instead, you throwing fits like this here."

I leaned against Hazel. "No. I ain't seeing him no more. I ain't seeing no doctor." The more I talked, the louder my voice rose. "I'll take Ruby and fix her myself." From behind me in the distance came the sound of heavy hoof beats. Samson. On the run. "Samson!" I screamed. "Run, M'dear!"

"Step over this guard." M'dear dropped the flashlight and grabbed my arm. I cried out, but M'dear pulled anyway. Dust settled on Samson's hooves as he stopped short at the cattleguard.

Hazel's sad, sad eyes watched me cradle her armful of calf outside the fence. "She's alright, Hazel." I wanted Hazel to not worry. I wasn't feeling any pain myself. I realized I hadn't thought about how bad I hurt since Hazel came for me.

A thin shaft of light touched the treetops past the pasture. "Guess we might as well go on down to Brother Blues'," said M'dear. "Ain't getting back inside that fence no time soon."

We walked a few steps down the road, and my legs started to falter. M'dear reached for Ruby. "Here. Let me carry the little one. We'll bind what skin's there together so's she won't hurt so bad. We'll use this here handkerchief. Let Brother Blues put on a good wrapping."

And we did.

Back home in the early light, I slipped an arm under Ruby's rib cage and another under her gut. I lifted her easy from the floor and placed her on the bed. Ruby looked strange with one leg stiffened out and bound while the other three bent in their natural way. Exhausted from the night before, I put on clean shorty pajamas and crawled into bed next to Ruby. I edged over and pulled her close. Ruby's bowed back fit into the curve of my body as if it belonged there. With the warmth of the calf next to me, I forgot for a moment about the throb that refused to leave my hip. My arms were better; the bandages M'dear had used had come off during Ruby's rescue. But my butt pounded with every heartbeat. It felt so hot that I longed to sit in a pond of cool water.

"Ruby," I whispered, "you can't grow, you know." I rubbed my hand over the calf's soft coat. "You grow and you'll have to go outside with the other heifers. Samson's out there, and he's one kind of bad dangerous." I scratched Ruby's ears. "Wild dogs, they out there, too. Some sorry old dog would love to have you for a midnight snack." I realized I was crying. "We got to figure some way to keep you from having to go back outside." I wiped my face and kissed Ruby's rubbery nose.

M'dear came in the room and walked to the edge of the bed. She sat for a moment before speaking. "What you telling this little calf, girl?"

"Nothing."

"You know you can't keep no calf inside of the house. Turn over here and look at me." M'dear tugged on my shoulder.

I rolled over and groaned.

"Hip still hurt?"

"Yessum. A bit." I had not told M'dear that my sore hips caused my legs to fail when I stood or walked a long way, but I figured she had some idea since our trip to Brother Blues' in the light of dawn.

"That why you're crying?"

"Ruby can't be let outside. Something might happen to her. She's lame and little and they's wild dogs out there and Samson. She can't run. How am I supposed to keep her safe?" As my words spilled out, so did my tears. M'dear slid over the sheet and held me close.

"We just peoples, Margaret Ann. Not much we can do about the nature of things. The living or dying."

I shied away. I didn't want to know this.

"Maybe we done wrong by saving this little girl. Maybe we done right. I ain't saying. I am saying that if the good Lord wants Ruby to grow to be a strong heifer, she will. He don't, she won't. It ain't our decision."

"It was us that saved her leg. She was hurting and crying. We couldn't leave her there. Wild dogs would've took her before light." I rubbed my hand over Ruby's nose. Ruby licked out her long tongue but couldn't reach me. "Or a bear."

"We ain't got no bear out here in the open like we are."

"Bear or not. You ain't saying we should've left her out there in the dark. Not helping Hazel at all."

"I ain't saying what we done was wrong. I'm saying I don't know if it was right. They ain't no clear answer."

"I ain't letting no wild animal tear her to pieces. I ain't letting Samson get to her. She's staying in here with me." I dropped across the calf's middle. Ruby bawled a grunt-like cry. "I'm sorry, Ruby," I said as I moved off the calf. "If I done wrong, I ain't seeing it. No matter what you say, M'dear."

"The house ain't no place to raise a heifer. She'll be so awful smelling we can't breathe. Here in my house, I don't know how long she can stay, Sugar Baby." M'dear walked to the door. "Take her out to the hay barn. We can come to some common ground on this later." She stepped into the living room.

I pulled the sheet over Ruby and rooted down beside her. "I won't let nothing happen to you, Ruby. You sleep now. We'll get you walking soon." Within the hour, Ruby let out gas like rolling thunder. I held my breath and swooped her up. When we laid down, I hadn't considered that Ruby might drop a cow patty in my bed. I hobbled through the house, weighted down by the calf. Two choices: the barn—way over yonder—or my treehouse—just off the porch. M'dear had said Ruby needed to nurse. M'dear promised that if Ruby couldn't nurse, she would fix her a bottle and one of us could feed her every half hour. I limped to the barn and laid her beside her mother. I fell asleep by her in the hay.

Chapter 15

Gladstone County Industrial and Trade School closes twice in the fall, one week for harvesting corn and one later for picking cotton. Christmas don't count. Both closing times meant I had holidays. I spent days following cattle trails and wandering into the low hills that surround the cattle pasture, Hazel right behind. Under scrub pines, needles made a brown floor to soften our steps. I tried to name each tree, each wildflower, and each bird by its song, even during the summer of the drought when most plants had died.

The year's corn pulling ended. I waited at Blues' store for the school bus. I'd been saying hello to Bailey Renfroe when Nell Hawkins popped out of the back of her daddy's barbershop and sashayed up to face me. "Where you been while's we in the fields?" It had been just a few weeks since she drew her brother's knife on me, but I had hoped she'd forgotten about me.

"Nowhere." I edged back. Nell was older than me and thirty pounds heavier.

"You think you better than us?" Nell smirked.

"Leave her be," said Bailey Renfroe. He moved a step closer.

I stammered out some nonsense.

Nell laughed. And she didn't stop with that one time. Her pestering got worse day by day. By the end of the week, Nell's laughing and pointy finger pushed me too far. I had to go back to the clinic after school. My body hurt. It was changing and I didn't like it. And I felt so ugly that day. I didn't want nobody messing with me. And now this. I didn't need no boy speaking up for me neither, even if it was Bailey Renfroe. I stepped back. Much like Samson had done when he was after my puppy, I lowered my head, took a strong run, and butted Nell Hawkins in the belly.

Nell dropped down, flat in the dirt. She gritted her teeth and pulled herself up, starting with her knees. Up she came. The taller Nell got, the more scared I got. I ran up the steps and banged on Brother Blues' screen door. "Let me in!" I called. "Please."

Brother Blues opened the door, his brow as furrowed as a sugarcane field. "What's going on here?"

"She's going to kill me." I slipped by Brother Blues and stood behind him, my hand fisted around his overalls leg. I was breathing through my mouth and couldn't stop.

Nell bounded on the porch, screaming, "I'm going to gouge your eyes out, you hussy you!"

Brother Blues put his arm out to stop Nell. "Stay outside, Nell. Need to settle this without calling Eb over."

Nell slumped down on the wooden bench next to Bailey Renfroe who had moved forward to save me. She talked to herself so that I had to strain to hear what she was talking about. Something about her brother being killed in Nam and him needing to be here to take care of her. I needed to remember to ask Brother Blues about all that. But Brother Blues towed me out to the porch by my arm. He stood between us two girls and waited for an explanation.

"I don't pick cotton. I don't pull corn. Ain't my fault M'dear don't send me." I watched Nell like a kitten cornered by a fox. "She ain't got no right to go on at me like that," I appealed to Brother Blues.

Blues turned to Nell. "Nell? What you got to say?"

"She butted my belly." Nell frowned. "She ought to know I got a baby."

"We all knows you got a baby." Brother Blues stepped closer to Nell. "That ain't no reason to gouge her eyes out."

"Yeah, but this one's different," Nell whimpered. "Going to name him Willie for my brother killed in Nam." I wondered how many times she had reminded us of that.

"Well." Brother Blues rubbed his chin with his big hand. "Seems to me that Margaret Ann could have hurt your baby when she butted you. You know Nell's going to have another baby?" He lowered his hand on my shoulder.

"Yes, but I don't want to hurt no baby." I wiped tears away with my forearm.

"Boo-hoo," whined Nell, like I was a crying baby myself.

"Wait here, you two," Brother Blues went into the store and came out with a tarnished teaspoon. "Solve this here and now. Margaret Ann, you first, since Nell started this. Take this spoon and gouge out one of Nell's eyes." He held the spoon out toward me.

I backed away. My hand shook. "I can't do that." I reached for the screen door handle. I heard the bus in the distance, bumping down the road. I imagined kids on the bus laughing at me for refusing the spoon. Calling me names like "scaredy cat" and "cry baby."

"Alright. Fair enough." He offered the spoon to Nell. "Here, Nell. Gouge out an eye. Either eye."

Nell's eyes widened. I waited for Nell to take the spoon and attack me. I squeezed my thighs so I wouldn't pee on myself. I had no place where I could run. Nell didn't move. The bus rumbled closer.

"What? Nobody wanting to gouge today?" Brother Blues' Adam's apple jiggled like he had swallowed a grin. "Guess I better put my spoon back, case we be needing it later." He entered the store as the bus brakes squealed. The bus stopped at the edge of the porch. The doors swished open. The thought came to me that I could stand up straight and breathe again now.

Nell never moved. "You go first."

I climbed up the steps, all the time watching Nell over my shoulder.

"Ain't you coming?" The bus driver yelled to Nell.

Nell flung back her head and stomped toward the open doors. Bailey Renfroe followed her. She sat in the seat behind me and whispered in my ear, "Nobody likes you."

I peeped out the window. There stood Hazel, only a thin barbed wire fence and the dirt road separating us. Hazel had seen it all. She nodded her heavy head in my direction. She was proud that I hadn't gouged out Nell's eye. I could tell.

Chapter 16

It was the Wednesday after the wreck, and I was back at school. I had avoided Nell Hawkins all week, but she saw me coming her way and smirked. She brought her fourteen-month-old son to school with her on Thursdays so her mother could clean houses in Prattville. Eb Hawkins believed the more schooling the better, even if the kid couldn't speak in sentences. A group of girls called Nell a "worldly woman" because she had survived birthing a child and was pregnant again. You would think they were a broke tail on a blue-tick hound, the way they trailed her. She kept them close so one would be handy if she wanted to escape the demands of a toddler who ran wide open through classrooms and down hallways. I saw her coming my way and turned up the stairs to the second floor.

I could tell I looked catching. Kids eyed my sores, especially the one on my face, and I turned away. Then I thought they were making fun of me by staring at me, but I realized now they had fear in their eyes, a dark, burning fear. I reflected this same fear back toward them because this fear of not knowing, not understanding, was eating me inside out.

I was six weeks into my blue jennies treatments. My old sores had closed with M'dear's doctoring, but new sores appeared from last week's shots. I walked with a crooked limp to keep my hips from throbbing. Nell saw me going down the hall. She struck.

"Yeller's got a zit," she sang down the hallway full of students.

Close enough to hear Nell's taunt and her followers laughing, I blinked back tears. Stupid Nell Hawkins and her gang. Vultures waiting to light and start their feed. I saw a vulture once when it ate a possum in the road, crippled but not good dead. Picking. Picking. Its hooked beak tearing open gaps where blood pumped out as steady as the cattle pond spring. My stomach turned. I swallowed hard so as not to puke on the floor.

I knew I had a zit. I had felt the tender spot when I washed my face the night before. I pulled out my mirror to study my face. Little red bumps covered my left cheek, but one on my right jaw had puffed up. That morning it had been festered, like the sores on my arms. It ached deep into my chin. I kept messing with it, rubbing it until it begged to bust. I hadn't had no shots near my face. But maybe the sores could spread on their own, like poison oak does. Touch it once and it's all over you.

The festered place was a puzzle. I couldn't ask Nurse. Nurse had never said a word to me, other than to tell me what to do. She just mostly wagged her finger as she looked at me from her dead gray eyes, motioning me to come on in or leave. Neither had Dr. Graves. I missed Miss Claire. I wanted her here. At school.

Helplessness came over me and I dragged my feet. Miss Claire, I needed her. I didn't want her to take me to get more shots—I wasn't going back for more shots. I said this every day. But I needed to have somebody to talk to about what was happening to my body. And I sure couldn't talk to Bailey Renfroe. He was a boy. And I needed somebody to protect me from Nell Hawkins. Bailey Renfroe was too round for that. Miss Claire would know things. She had been to college, and she worked at the Free Women's Clinic. Most telling, she had been so gentle and kind every time she took me to the clinic. Nice even about the wreck that Friday.

I changed my direction, as I said, and went up the stairwell. At the landing, the stairs made a sharp shift to the right. I slipped. I caught myself before I fell backwards down the stairs. My books hit the floor with a thud that echoed down both floors. I sat for a moment while my head settled. I had never been dizzy before. I pounded my fist against the floor and pulled myself up so I wouldn't be late for class.

Standing made my head throb. It came to me that my head had hurt for days now, and I had ignored it. But today the pain cut like sharp knives across my forehead. I sat down again to gather myself. Some teacher down the hall rang a hand bell announcing that I was late. A tardy meant time after school. Time after school meant I would miss my bus home.

Throw your own self down these stairs, I thought. But then I realized that I might do no more than conk my head. *If I tumble down, I want to be dead at the bottom. Nell Hawkins will be scared then for sure.*

None of it mattered. I had not felt good since the shots started. Over the past weeks, I thought more and more that I didn't like myself much anyway. I made a list of all the things I hated about myself. It read like the lists of ingredients Mrs. Garret had us make when we learned a new recipe: jitters, headaches, body throbs, zits, arm and butt sores, dizziness, and lots of hate. Hate. Hate for myself.

That day, I only wanted to sit on the stairs and cry. I wanted Baa with me. My face hurt. Not the way kids out of meanness say "Yo face so ugly, it must hurt," but deep down aching from poison inside my head. Some could have whispered about my face hurting. I was monster ugly.

There had been that day when Nell Hawkins said it out loud. She came up to me and told me, nose to nose. Saying it made it true. Maybe she meant my face was so ugly that it hurt her to look at it. I don't know. Even now, I try not to think about it.

Chapter 17

Tears came without my permission. I buried my head in my arms and bawled. Why did I have to go to class anyway? I would be stuck in Hyssop all my life, like everybody else in this sorry school. I would iron like M'dear and live in a pasture full of stinking heifers and bulls. I probably stink myself. I lifted my right arm and sniffed. The movement made my upper arm throb. Carrying books didn't help. It didn't matter if I stunk or not. Nobody got close enough to smell me if I did. Not with that lowdown Nell Hawkins around.

I wiped my face with the front of my skirt. I stacked my books out of the way on the top stair and walked out the double doors of Gladstone County Industrial and Trade School. I was finished. Nothing here for me. Nobody saw me leave.

I glared back at the school's name. The sign should call the school for what it is. "That Colored School." That's what everybody called it, like it was painted orange or yellow or purple or some other gaudy color. The only person I heard call it by its real name was M'dear.

Outside, the sun burned the top of my head worse than the day of the wreck. The heat or the distance home hadn't occurred to me when I walked out. Walking to Brother Blues' store from home, that mile, didn't seem so long, but walking the miles and miles back through Sweetwater and on into Hyssop and on to home, I didn't know. Walking to the moon and back might have been easier.

The dirt road took a sharp turn to the right. To the left ran a rutted road I hadn't noticed before. Withered weeds down its center tried to thrive. The road called to me, "*Come this way. I know a short cut.*" I listened to the worn road and took it.

Sweat ran from my temples and down my neck. It dripped into my eyes. I blinked hard, but my eyes burned from the salt, burned bad. At first, I tried to wipe the sweat away. After a few hundred yards, I gave up. I wanted water. My mouth was so dry, my tongue felt furry. Rain had been so long in coming that not a trickle of fresh water wet the bottom of the ditch.

At the next bend, all I could see was row after row of corn plants, squatty and covered with small ears packed against the stalks. It would be several months before coloreds would be out pulling. I would stay home and spend my time with Hazel and Ruby. This picking season, I might thread chinaberry seeds and make myself a necklace.

If it had rained this summer there would have been flowers along this road—weeds topped with small purple flowers that reached my knees and wild carrots M'dear called Queen Anne's lace with their flat white blooms, round as a saucer. Later, goldenrod would droop their heavy heads. Hyssop would be in full bloom. And bees. Bees would be everywhere.

Back toward the horizon, no trees appeared, no shade. I needed shade. If I walked into the field and lay among the cornstalks, I would get no relief from the sun. My dizziness had come back. I swallowed hard not to throw up. I walked on and walked on, stumbling now and then.

Cornstalk shadows moved across the ground. Corn that should have towered over me stood no taller than my chest. The sun was leaning toward the west, and I stopped to gather my bearings. All I saw was corn, row after row after stunted row. No house. No barn. No water. I was lost. Thinking about how long I had walked, I reasoned that going back wouldn't help. School would be closed; my bus gone. When I didn't get off that bus and walk on home, M'dear would be so mad she could spit nails. Not that M'dear would lift a hand. She never lifted a hand to me—except the time Bailey Renfroe and me got drunk. That wasn't M'dear's way.

I wished Bailey Renfroe had come with me. He would know more about not getting lost than me since he's a boy. I wished Hazel had come with me, but she couldn't leave Ruby. Maybe Ruby would be sleeping and Hazel could float over the fields, drop out of the clouds, and land right here beside me and lead me back home.

I sat in the dust. I buried my face in my knees and muttered, "Somebody come find me. Please." I looked around to see if anybody had appeared. The fields were as empty as before. I bowed my head and, in case M'dear was right about saying it out loud, I spoke. "Hello, God. It's me. I messed up and got myself lost. Should I know this cornfield? Is this my punishment for not towing a sack? Nell Hawkins would say so."

I rubbed my forehead. "I hurt so bad. What've I done to be so different? Nobody likes me but Bailey Renfroe. Me and Bailey Renfroe, we're odd man out. You know him. I'm going to marry him, but you know that." A fat mosquito buzzed my ear. "Brother Blues says you can do everything. Can you fly Hazel over here to stay with me? She likes me like nobody else but M'dear. I'll close my eyes and wait for you to decide."

I closed my eyes and waited. Nothing happened. Nothing but no-see-ums moved. No Hazel. I patted my pockets for a handkerchief. Nothing to wipe the sweat off my face.

My head went around and around, and out of the blue sky floated a voice. "Odom?"

It was Bailey Renfroe. I swiveled my head around to find him, but nobody was in sight.

"Odom," the voice called again. I stood up.

"Where you at, Bailey Renfroe?" I yelled. "Why you not on the bus going home?"

"Look for me later," the voice said.

"What you mean? Where am I to look?" All the time I was looking here and there. Up and down. No Bailey Renfroe.

"In the dust."

"What?"

"Look for me in the dust." It repeated itself. "I'll be there, Odom, when you need me more."

I had to sit down. I was going crazy. Ain't nobody found in dust. Besides, I needed him now. What could be worse than being lost and by yourself?

A cold shiver ran over my body there in the cornfield. My hands shook and my knees refused to lift my weight. I had been scared when I saw that I was lost, but Bailey Renfroe's talking to me out of nowhere terrified me. I spun around trying to spot somebody. Nobody around but me. I closed my eyes and waited for him to talk again. He didn't.

Chapter 18

The afternoon that I ran away from school, I sat in the narrow rut until my head cleared. My brain peeped out questions that I didn't want to answer. I couldn't answer them. *What will M'dear do to me? Probably take away my time with Hazel.* That would be the worst. Not being able to cuddle with Hazel as she chews her hay. Not leaning against Hazel's solid body and scratching her behind her ears.

"But none of that matters," I said out loud. "Unworthy, that's what I am. Unworthy and unlovable. And ugly. Itchy pimples on my face. My hair refusing to kink as much as the other girls'. I'll sit here and sweat it out. Starve or thirst to death in this hellish heat."

There, I had said it. I said "hellish." I yelled "hellish" one more time to make it more true.

Brother Blues would not approve. He might not let me come into his store church. I'd be cast out. M'dear would be mortified. Nobody would send her ironing anymore. She wouldn't have no money to live on. It would all be my fault. All 'cause I ran away from school and thirsted to death in the middle of a cornfield.

I'm not a sharecropper, so I never dragged a cotton sack into fields at break of day. I never pulled corn. It would be right that I died in a cornfield. I already made myself into an outcast by having sores that showed on my face. Memories of the scapegoats in the sacrifice stories of the Old Testament proved me right. Send them out with the sins on their backs and let them die in the desert. "That's me!" I yelled to the endless sky. "A black and white goat by my own self in the desert."

A crow circled overhead. It cried out *caw, caw, caw*. I watched it play on high air currents for a time, and then I hefted myself off the dirt. Crows eat anything. I didn't want a crow eating my dead body. I'd follow the crow. Crows go in a straight line. They always going somewhere else. They didn't follow roads. They took shortcuts over fields, over trees.

The crow took me through six more fields. For a time, I tried to trot with it, but it flew faster than I could go. Then in the distance appeared a stand of pine only a few years old, row on row, meant for somebody's harvesting. The crow soared over the treetops and disappeared. If I couldn't keep up, I could at least watch the sky for my crow and head in that direction.

Entering the dappled pine shade, I breathed deep the scent of sap and pine mold. I sneezed it out. Straw covering the ground begged me to sit and rest, but if I did I would lose my crow. So I jogged along. After a time, I coughed a dry cough. And coughed again. My nose took in more mold and tried to sneeze it out, but I swallowed and coughed harder. I had to stop to breathe. "Oh, God," I prayed, "don't let me step on no copperhead. They do love pine straw so."

Standing under the pines, I threw back my head. Treetops had grown so high they seemed to be freakish green umbrellas that refused to break the sun's heat. I bent over, my hands on my thighs. I breathed deep and deep again until I had charge of my lungs and could travel on. Something moved in the straw on my left. I was sure of it. Then my legs gave way. I dropped to my knees. "Out of my way, you copperheads."

I vomited out my headache. It left a nasty bitter taste in my mouth and throat, but relief spread through my body. Then my mind tilted. Such thirst and headache throbs had made the knots from the shots less painful. Now with the headache gone, my arms and hip pounded harder. I stood and rubbed my upper arms. From a skinny pine ahead, my crow took flight. I hurried in its direction.

I smelled stagnant water before I saw the river. The edge of the pine grove opened to the bank of the Buckhorn. I garnered my strength and crashed through scratchy weeds. Fear told me I had to run. A saw briar reached out and grabbed my leg, ripping it open. Warm blood trickled down my calf and into my shoe. I hopped several steps to regain my stride, trying to ignore the burn from the briar cut. Reaching the brink of the Buckhorn, I walked over dirt that had cracked in irregular patterns and curled at the edges. Once I reached the middle of the river's bed, I fanned tiny hoverflies away from the water's surface and then fell into the warm, narrow flow, face-first.

Unable to breathe under water, I turned over and laid in the muck, my clothes and body soaking up the rank water until the sting from the saw briar let up and weakness left my legs.

Sitting up, I inhaled a hot breeze. It was strong enough to flatten my blouse against my chest. I splashed stinking water on my face, but the warm water did little to cool my burning sores. I lifted my hair from my neck and shook out the water. One twist and it fell back into place. I dug out mud from the river bottom and patted each sore, even the one on my jaw. The mud caked as soon as I took my hand away. I stood and searched the clouds for rain. The color of old bruises, they spoke of rain, but promised nothing.

In the near distance, a car passed on the road. I got up and walked toward the sound. Across Buckhorn River on a low rise sat the house. I breathed out a quiet "Ohhhh." I had never seen a house so big, so fancy. It was the house. My mouth watered at the thought of living in such a house. I had heard of the house on the school bus, but I had never seen it. I turned my back to the house. It was not a house built for coloreds or kids. No swing. No treehouse. Not even a barn.

I stepped out of the river and crossed a low hill. I grasped a spindly pine sapling and used it to climb the bank rope-like up to a concrete bridge. The mud on my arms crackled and dropped off in little chunks. A fancy black mailbox at the top of the rise read "Bullard." I didn't need to read no name. I knew as soon as I saw it that it was my daddy's house.

Had somebody seen me come out of the riverbed with my fists stuck together with pinesap, hair soggy and dress clinging to my body, he would have declared that he had seen a demon materialize from the dust of the river.

I had to get home. I walked the unpaved road, the sun at my back. I tried to wipe the sap from my hands. Rather than coming off, it stuck harder. I had to open my hands by unlocking my fingers one by one.

What I would tell M'dear about running away? I had no idea. Since I'd been going to the clinic, a weary lonesomeness had overcome me and told me to get the hell out of there. I smiled. Thinking the forbidden word gave me again a sense of power. I could do whatever I wanted. I could think whatever I wanted. I had done both. Maybe it wasn't so good, this cussing. Now it had me facing a direction I had never thought I would have to take.

Chapter 19

I dragged on toward the coming dark. The rotten smell of river water in my clothes and hair surrounded me like a haze. A rumbling sound from behind said *"Thunder on the horizon."* I took a quick look over my shoulder. Not comfortable with walking backwards, I stumbled. What I saw sent me looking for a place to hide. There were no trees. No houses. Not even a big bush. A Black girl walking down a White man's road would bode no good.

But I walked on. I made believe I never heard the sound. But I had. The motor's roar came closer. Again, I looked over my shoulder. It was still there. A farm truck, a dreary black. Somebody had cut the back down so that its low wooden rails held barrels safe against falling. A truck so big it took up the road and it was racing right at me.

I jumped into the shallow ditch. Pain stabbed my body when I landed. I bit my lip. I would not cry.

Spiky weeds and ditch dust clouded my sight. Everything around me changed to dense grays and brown. This was no good. If I wanted to get rid of this misery, I had to meet it head on. I couldn't keep running. I stepped back into the road and turned to face the truck, eyes closed, arms dangling at my sides. "You don't scare me!" I screamed.

The truck screeched to a stop. A shower of fine grime settled over me. I coughed and tasted dirt. Blood pulsed through my head. I gulped and opened my eyes. A dull, silver grille, taller than me, rattled so close I could reach out and touch it. The engine's heat swished over my body, air hotter than what I faced in the cotton fields. My hands quivered. My whole body shook. Here was death itself, right in front of me, nose to nose. All the anger, pain and fear I had tried to hide for weeks and weeks ran down my face in tears.

A White man jumped out of the cab and rushed to grab me. "Girlie?" he said. "What're you doing on this road? And by yourself? Don't you know. . . ?"

I knew it was Mr. Gibbons, but I couldn't look at him. Hypnotized by the truck grille, I stared through Mr. Gibbons.

"Speak to me, girl." Mr. Gibbons shook my shoulders until my eyes focused.

"I peed," I choked through the tears. A small puddle of wet lay between my feet.

"Seeing you there in the road like some lost ghost almost made me pee on myself, too," Mr. Gibbons walked over and opened the passenger door to the cattle truck. "Get in and I'll ride you on home."

I couldn't move. It astonished me that something as common as a truck grille could take out a life. Death now mattered in a way other than my puppy and Bailey Renfroe's granny being buried. It demanded my respect in a way I hadn't considered. I whispered, "No."

"Get in, I say."

I ran my hands through my hair. "I best ride in the back." I moved away. "This ain't my road." I knew it was true.

"No such thing. Get in this here truck. It's nigh on to dark and I only got one tail light. I don't need no State Trooper rolling up behind me."

Still dazed, I staggered past the open door and around the back of the truck. Fifty-gallon drums filled the bed. Water had sloshed over the tops and dripped from the truck bed into the dust. The water smelled like the most delicious water I had ever known. "Can I have a taste of this water? It's awful hot."

"I ain't got a dipper, but you can climb up and use your hands." Mr. Gibbons shook his head like he might be confused. "With this heavy load, it's a wonder I got this truck stopped before running clean over you."

Ignoring my wet skirt, Mr. Gibbons lifted me up to the truck bed. I put my face in the closest barrel and drank. The water, though warm, soothed the sores on my face. I wanted more than anything to climb into the water and soak away the pain from my body.

"Come on, now. That's enough." Mr. Gibbons probably didn't want me to falter like some overworked horse. He helped me to the ground and in the truck. He cranked the motor.

He later told M'dear that, when he looked over at me, I sat there staring, my eyes empty. He said he thought I didn't know where I was. "Her hands in her lap, their palms up like they was waiting for something to drop into them, they lay limp as a wet rag," he had said.

Later, I spied from my treehouse in my china-berry tree. M'dear would tell Mr. Gibbons what I had told her—that I was walking home from school and got lost. That I found the Buckhorn River and climbed up to the bridge. I had been this road before. On the school bus.

Mr. Gibbons told her that I hadn't told all the truth. He knew. He recognized terror in my eyes. "Something bad's happening with this child," he said. "Somebody ought to bear witness."

"Ought to go to the principal. Get this Nell Hawkins out of the way."

"Tomorrow's Friday. Keep her home. Give her the weekend to overcome what's happening to her." Mr. Gibbons thought a minute. "Might try myself to talk to that social worker and Blues about the wreck last week."

I left them talking. I needed Hazel and Ruby. I slipped around the back of the house to the barn. Inside, I missed the mud from the river. I had mudded my sores good, but M'dear had washed off what hadn't dropped off on its own. I ran a hand down my upper arm. The lumps and pus pockets were still there. I ignored the prickly hay and lay down beside Ruby where she slept next to her mother. M'dear found me after dark.

Part II

Chapter 20

A week had passed since wrecking the jeep and learning about Margaret Ann's sores. I was driving my daddy's old Studebaker truck, but not to the clinic. I was going to Montgomery for information. My employer, Hank Bullard, not only owned the Free Women's Clinic, but also every drugstore in Prattville. I couldn't risk word of my mission traveling back to him, at least not until I found what I was looking for.

As the miles went by, I thought back to the interview that had led to my job at the clinic. It had been a short interview. I knew without question that Hank Bullard was a man with a purpose. The more he talked, the more I agreed with his rationale. He was quick spoken, to the point of being abrupt. The job at Free Women's Clinic would be to research people who couldn't afford health care, especially the coloreds and poor Whites, find them, and bring them to the clinic for treatment. Some might come once a week; some, only one time.

"Coloreds don't react to medicine like we do, Claire," Mr. Bullard said. "Dr. Graves will decide how many times a patient comes and when."

"What you describe is exactly what I want to accomplish in my work, Mr. Bullard," I said.

"Call me 'Hank,'" he said quickly before continuing. "You answer to Dr. Graves and Dr. Graves only. He knows what we need done. And you have to sign a statement of confidentiality, you understand?"

"Of course. That's one of the key tenets of social work. I learned that right away at the university." I tugged at my suit's straight skirt where my knees were bulging through the polyester. I felt a blush creep up my neck. *He mustn't think me inattentive.*

His voice turned raspy. "Talk to anybody about anything that happens in this clinic and you won't work in this county again. I'll even see that you won't work in this state again. Understand?"

I bit the inside of my lip to hide my shock. Had he just threatened me? I needed the job. The pay was fair, as much as any beginning salary, and I had college loans to pay off. I needed a good car, not my daddy's rattle-trap truck. I wasn't on good terms with my parents, especially my mother, who had not wanted me to become a social worker. I wanted a place of my own. Flat out, I needed money. I worked up a weak smile and nodded my head.

"Say it." Bullard leaned over his desk into my face. "Say it, Whitehurst, or you don't get the job."

"Yes, sir." I resisted the urge to wipe my sweaty palms on my skirt. "I understand, Mr. Bullard— Hank. No word about the clinic, doctor, nurses, or patients can be spoken outside clinic walls." I rearranged my hair.

"See that you remember. Be at the clinic Monday at 7:30, and Doc will show you the files. You can start there."

I gripped the chair arms to steady my legs as I rose. At the door, I reached for the knob to find his hand already there. I had not expected him to open the door for me. I had not heard him move across the room. Out from behind the desk, he was a different man. Less intimidating. But I told myself I had no need to worry about a handsome man. I would be working directly with the doctor. All Mr. Bullard had to do was sign my check.

I shook my head as I pulled into downtown Montgomery. What exactly had I subjected Margaret Ann, and possibly other girls, to in exchange for my paycheck?

I stopped at the third drugstore I saw. Mother always told me threes were lucky. Maybe so. I had my questions ready.

I entered the drugstore and walked to where the pharmacist stood behind a chin-high counter. I stood on tiptoe and asked if I could speak privately with him about symptoms my "sister" was having. Within a few minutes, I had described Margaret Ann's sores, before and after the impetigo I had noticed on her face, her withdrawal and depression. "I'm afraid she might want to kill herself," I whispered. "I need to know what the medicine is."

"Shots or pills?" he asked.

"Shots," I said. "Once a week, sometimes more."

"Age?"

"Twelve, almost thirteen," I said.

"Why is she getting the shots?"

"I have no idea."

"She really your sister?" He bent forward so no one could hear our conversation.

"Why do you ask?" I bit my lower lip.

"Might you have some idea about the medicine?" He cocked his head.

"No. I was hoping you might."

The pharmacist shook his head and ran his hand through thin grey hair. "No offense intended, young lady, but is your sister colored?"

I flushed. My knees buckled. I grabbed a shelf. Two bottles of magnesia fell to the floor, and I scrambled to put them back. When I looked again at the pharmacist, I caught a half-smile, as if he were teasing me.

"Most girls like you come in here wanting some new birth control pill. I tell them you got to have a prescription." He chuckled. "The way they slink out of here tells me they been playing at being married." He scratched his scalp. "Don't think I ever had anybody ask about what you're asking."

I stammered. I put my hands in my pants pockets and clinched my fists. "She's not my sister. She's my friend. I've been taking her to a women's clinic, and she's getting worse every day. Somebody's got to stop it. I need to know what they're giving her so I can at least tell her mother." Breathless, I looked back at the pharmacist and blinked back tears. "I feel responsible."

"I don't know what they're giving her, but sounds like it might be a shot that shuts down the ovaries. It's not FDA approved. In fact, it's classified as 'experimental.'" The pharmacist took a pen from his shirt pocket and wrote the name on a small piece of paper. "If it's that, somebody is using an illegal form of birth control on this girl." He handed me the paper. "You do need to tell her mother. And yes, she might try suicide. Others have." He set his lips into a straight line and turned away.

I nearly stumbled as I walked back outside. I had trouble finding the key to crank the truck and then dropped it on the floorboard I laid my head on the rough steering wheel to control my shaking. *What have I done? Been part of something evil.*

Then I raised my head, my teeth gritted. I had to fix it. "Illegal" the pharmacist had said. I could report it to the newspaper. Tell them everything I knew.

A police car passed slowly by the truck, and my breath got caught in my throat. I ducked my head guiltily, the possible consequences of the role I had played in all this dawning on me. Just because I had been ignorant until now didn't mean I was safe. All I ever wanted with this job was to help people, and I had thought that I was helping the girls by taking them to the clinic, that I was making their lives better.

Tears rolled down my cheeks as I mumbled, "I failed."

Chapter 21

"What if it had been me, Mama?"
After learning what Dr. Graves was giving Margaret Ann, by Monday morning, I knew it was time to speak.

"But what if it had been me?"

Loretta cracked an egg on a cup's lip. She let the egg plop into the empty cup, eyed the yolk, and tossed the broken egg into the trash. "Damn," she said and wiped her fingers on her apron. She took another, cracked its shell, and dropped it into the same cup. She swirled the egg around and poured it into Aunt Lucille's old crockery bowl, the cream-colored one with blue and pink borders.

"Set out the plates. Breakfast is almost ready," Mama said.

"Are you listening to me?" I demanded.

"Take that dishrag and wash off the table. See if you can get that blackberry jam stain out of the enamel." Loretta cracked another egg and threw it into the trash.

I wiped the table and walked around to take on the purplish brown splotch. I rubbed hard, pressing strength from my shoulders to loosen the discoloration. "It's not coming out," I said. "It's been here too long."

Loretta threw away another egg.

"Why are you throwing away so many eggs?" I asked as I straightened out the dishrag to dry.

"They's ruint," Loretta said. "Yolks got a spot of blood. Ever' other one."

I stepped to the counter to see. "That blood just means they're fertile. You can still use them."

"I ain't feeding my family no egg with blood in it," Loretta said. "It ain't natural." She took a whisk from the cabinet drawer and beat the eggs, slowly at first, to mix the yolk and white, then faster, harder, as if she were angry at the eggs. Metal clinked against the bowl's sides.

"Geez, Mama. You're leaving black streaks in Aunt Lucille's bowl." I brushed my hair back from my face, combing my bangs with my fingers.

"I got to get them whiter. They's better that way." Loretta kept her back to me and continued to beat.

"And I got to do what I think is right." I fingered the edge of the dishrag and moved it to the sink.

"Check that toaster. Your daddy don't like dark toast." Loretta beat on.

I released the toaster lever. Two slices of bread, still white, popped up. I pushed the control back down for the slices to brown. "They're no more than babies. Little girls, really. Have you thought on that?"

Loretta forked bacon from the skillet and poured the bowl of pale egg mixture into grease too hot for scrambling. Scorched scalloped edges lifted from the heat.

"My meeting's at 9:00." I stepped in front of my mother. "Somebody's got to say it out loud."

Loretta slammed down her spatula. "Claire . . ." she began and reconsidered. "What've you got on? You look like a hippy in that droopy skirt."

I breathed deep. "After my meeting, I'm going to go to the clinic and quit. I need to be comfortable to say what I've got to say."

"You stood too long at that liberal university," muttered Loretta.

"Mama, I'm not letting it lie." I picked up Aunt Lucille's bowl from the counter and caressed its sides.

"Let what lie?" Loretta picked up the spatula and wiped the counter clean of egg.

"The job," I said. "I'm reporting the whole bunch." I put a fresh dishcloth in the bottom of the sink and set the bowl on it. "You haven't listened to a word I've said."

"Not you. People will know it come from you. Lose your job." Mama stepped around me. "Neighbors won't speak to us."

"I'm quitting, Mama. I just said that. Soon as I leave the meeting with the reporter."

"What reporter?"

"A reporter from the *Montgomery Advertiser*." I followed her across the room. "I won't be part of this now I know what's going on." I reached up and handed down a bowl. "My God, it's 1968, not 1938. Alabama's not Nazi Germany."

Loretta took the bowl. "It's not your problem, Claire." She set the bowl on the stove and reached for a hug.

I gripped my fists and white knuckles appeared. I was all out of hugs. Behind my mother, smoke rose from the toaster. "Daddy's toast is burning."

"Don't be coming back 'round here crying because you got no place else to go. Your daddy finds out, you won't be putting your feet under his table again. Remember that."

I felt my jaw lock. I picked up the keys to the old farm truck and walked toward the door.

"That damn college done made you uppity." Loretta grabbed Aunt Lucille's old crockery. She drew back to throw the bowl, but she set the bowl gently on the kitchen counter and reached into the loaf for two more slices of white bread.

I closed the door real quiet.

Chapter 22

I stayed home with M'dear Thursday through Monday. I thought hard about never going back to the colored school. Not going to school nowhere. Never again. M'dear had done that. Why couldn't I?

Late Monday afternoon, I heard steps on the gravel. I moved to the window and sat sideways so I could spy.

I knew who it was without seeing his face. Waddling from being round all over, he had to be Bailey Renfroe. He was letting his hair grow into an afro, like the high school kids. All that hair made his neck disappear. He eased up to the porch and glanced around. He put my books on the floor and laid a bunch of brown sticks on top. He started back to the cattle-guard.

I stuck my head out the window and called, "Hey there, Bailey Renfroe."

He stopped.

"Meet me on the porch. Got something to show you." I'll never be able to explain what got into me to call Bailey Renfroe back or do what I did next. It was like a voice that was not mine came out of my mouth.

Bailey Renfroe met me on the porch with the sticks in his hand.

"What's that?" I asked.

"Hyssop. The Good Book says it'll heal. Brother Blues, he say so."

"It's dead." I put the sticks to my nose and smelled. Nothing but dust. "Do I need healing?"

"Don't know. This is all I could find." He hung his head. "Just in case."

I could see I had hurt his feelings, so I took the sticks and laid them back on my books. I motioned for him to come inside. He shook his head. I grabbed his hand to keep him from dashing away.

Bailey Renfroe shook his head again, hard this time. "I ain't."

I tugged him on. When I opened the door and moved aside so Bailey Renfroe could see for himself, his eyes grew wide. "Oh my god, you got a bull calf sleeping on your bed." He pinched his nose. "Geez, he stinks."

"Yep." I grinned. "Well, no. She's a heifer. Hazel's." After a moment, I added, "And mine. I bring her in here after she feeds and shits so's she can sleep quiet." I leaned near his ear. "Can you keep a secret?"

Bailey shrugged his boxy shoulders. "I guess so."

I drew him close and clasped my hands on his arms. "You got to help me hide her."

"I don't know." He stared at the sleeping calf. "How long she been here?"

"Off and on since she cut her leg. She's already getting too big to stay in here." I stroked Ruby's back. "Mr. Gibbons'll come around soon asking where she at." I towed Bailey Renfroe toward the bed. "You got to help."

Ruby lay on her side, her three good legs tucked under her body. Her bandaged leg stuck out and hung over the side of the bed. Her head tucked against her side and her tail hidden beneath her back legs, she was beautiful. "Ain't she an awful mess of gentleness?" I smiled.

"She stay put?" Bailey Renfroe asked.

I nodded. "She can't go nowhere with her leg hurt. At night, I leave her with Hazel and fluff her hay up good." I rubbed my hand over Ruby's forehead. Her orangy coat held my handprint. "But she's already getting heavy. And she don't rest long. I ain't getting too much sleep taking her to the hay barn and back every time she wants to nuss."

"How's she eat?" Bailey whispered.

"I take her to Hazel and hold her up because she can't stand up good. Or I give her cow's milk in a bottle. With a nipple."

"Where you plan to hide her?" Bailey took a quick look around the room. "No place in here to hide a calf."

"We going to hoist her up into my treehouse and put a board over the door so she won't fall out." I licked my lips. I needed a glass of Kool-Aid to wet my throat.

Bailey Renfroe spoke louder now. "What if'n we drop her?" Bailey wrung his hands. "You said she's heavy."

"She ain't all that heavy," I argued. "You carry the tail end and I'll carry her head so we won't hurt her cut leg."

Bailey Renfroe backed away.

"You got to do this. You said you could hold a secret." I tapped my foot on the floor so he would know that I meant it. "Come on. We ain't got much time. M'dear'll be back from Brother Blues' in a bit."

"She know she's here?"

"'Course she does. She just don't know I keep bringing her inside. She won't know where she went to." I stuck my chin out. "We're losing time. Let's go."

"What if she kicks me?"

"Ruby ain't never kicked nobody," I lied, but it was just a little white lie. He wouldn't understand that Ruby had kicked me when she hurt, that girls do that. I slipped my arm under Ruby's head and lifted her shoulders. Ruby licked my arm. "You get hold of your end."

Bailey slid his arm under Ruby's hindquarters. He smiled as he lifted the calf's weight. "She ain't heavy as I thought."

We walked side by side toward the door. I held the hurt leg steady. When we reached the door, we looked at each other. We were too wide to pass through the door jam. Bailey Renfroe had a question all over his face. "Turn sideways, silly." I sniggered.

Moving Ruby through the house and across the yard raised no problems. Climbing the three steps up called for more thinking. Bailey Renfroe lifted his half of Ruby and laid the weight on my shoulder. He took my half and, from behind, placed it at the back of my neck and laughed. Pain stabbed my hip and my knees weakened.

"What's funny?" I snorted.

"You look like you got a orange wrap around your neck," Bailey Renfroe said between giggles.

"Hush up. Help push me up the ladder so I won't fall backwards," I ordered.

Bailey Renfroe put a hand on each of my hips and shoved the lumps made by the clinic shots.

"Ow," I moaned.

Bailey Renfroe dropped his hands and stepped back.

"No. Don't listen to me. Just do it."

I struggled up a ladder rung. Then another. As Bailey Renfroe hoisted, I climbed all three steps until I reached the floor of the treehouse. I bent forward and let Ruby rest where she lay. Ruby cried a woeful mooing, over and over.

"Ain't going to work, Odom." Bailey Renfroe bent over, his hands on his knees as he spoke between gasps. "She's wanting her mama. Or you. Up there with her."

"Let's get her down and take her to the hay barn."

"Shoot. We just got her up there." Bailey Renfroe sat on the ground, "tired" written all over his face.

"Three steps ain't much. 'Sides, I can lift her up and drop her down. You catch her. But don't let her leg hit the ground." I climbed the steps before Bailey could argue. I sat on the treehouse floor, edged Ruby into my lap and held her out over the steps. "She's heavy all right." Ruby licked my ear. "Quit it, Ruby." I tilted my head away from her and laughed. "She's coming on three. Be ready."

Bailey Renfroe stood up. "This ain't going to work."

"One. Two." Ruby squirmed against my hold. My hands slipped, and Ruby slid out of my arms. She landed smack on Bailey Renfroe. Her full weight put both of them on the ground with a whomp.

"You hurt?" I asked. "Ruby hurt?"

"Get down here and get this cow offen me." Bailey Renfroe lay flattened to the ground under the calf.

"She ain't no cow. She can't be a cow until she drops a calf herself." I stepped down the stairs, talking with my back to Bailey Renfroe. "Don't you know nothing?"

Ruby gave out a moaning sound.

"I know you one crazy girl. That's for sure." Bailey Renfroe sounded real aggravated.

With the bandaged leg, Ruby couldn't get up by herself. With the calf laying on his gut, Bailey Renfroe couldn't get up neither. I lifted Ruby so he could rise. "Come on. We'll make her a hidey hole in the hay barn."

"I don't know," protested Bailey Renfroe. "Not another dumb scheme, Odom." He brushed dirt from his pants.

I rolled my eyes. "Don't whine. Just help me get her to the hay barn." Bailey Renfroe could be so ornery.

Inside the barn, Ruby rested on scattered hay. I said how to stack the bales of hay. We built a cave-like place in the back corner, so we only had to create one full wall and one half-wall, leaving a space for Hazel to come and go. The walls were tall enough to hide Hazel, and tall enough to exhaust both of us. When finished, we placed Ruby on a low mound of hay against the barn's solid wall so she would feel safe.

Hazel waited at the barn doors. She didn't need to be shown her calf. She trotted into the hay cave and nudged Ruby with her black nose. I held Ruby steady as she nursed. Bailey Renfroe sat in the barn's entrance, breathing in hot dry air. His flushed face begged for water.

After Ruby finished feeding, I came out. Me and Bailey Renfroe collapsed on the ground. I put my hand on his leg. "Thanks for bringing my books."

"Yeah."

"And the hyssop."

We shuffled back to the porch and laid down across the planks. Bailey Renfroe, with his arms flung up and away from his body like he was ready to fly away, fell straight to sleep. I laid on my stomach, my face turned toward the road, and dangled my left arm off the side of the porch. That's how M'dear found us.

Chapter 23

Nigh on to dusk, Mr. Gibbons entered the barn and called out, "Best you come down here, girlie."

I slid further back under the hay. Disturbing the dry dust made me sneeze.

"Come on down now. I know you're up there. You don't want me to have to come get you."

"Not coming down," I said and added, "Sir."

"And why not?"

I edged to the loft's drop-off and watched him. As usual, he placed his forefinger against one nostril and blew snot into the hay. The smell of manure and dry hay always tickled his nose. Hazel, her chin held up like she ruled the land, stood beside the wall of hay bales.

"I got on a dress. Go out the barn door first."

Mr. Gibbons shuffled across the ground. I

backed down the rickety ladder, hit the ground and pressed down the skirt of my dress. "You can come on back in now, Mr. Gibbons."

He turned from facing the outside field and walked toward me. "I done told you, you can't keep coming in this barn. Make one skittish move and one of these heifer's going to trample you."

"I only come to Hazel's stall. She won't hurt me. I come to feed her."

"From that hay loft?" He nodded his head toward the ceiling.

I picked a fist-full of hay off the ground. "Mr. Gibbons, you know my daddy." I spoke with knowing, rather than asking.

"Why do you say that?" Mr. Gibbons removed his Braves cap and combed his fingers through his hair.

"M'dear says you bring money from him. For me and her." I stretched a hay-filled hand toward Hazel.

"I didn't come down here to talk about your daddy. I come to talk about Hazel's calf."

I put the hay under Hazel's nose. Hazel tugged at the wad until I opened my hand. Her thick black tongue wrapped around the hay and pulled it into her mouth. She ground her big, square teeth side to side.

"Girlie," Mr. Gibbons stepped into the stall, blocking my way out. "What happened to Hazel's calf?"

I bent for more hay. "What happened to my daddy?"

Mr. Gibbons stopped my hand mid-air. "The calf, Margaret Ann."

I pulled back my hand. "You don't know Margaret Ann."

"I know you, girlie. And I know you know more than you're telling about that calf." He crossed his arms and stared at me.

I laid my face against Hazel's velvety nose. "Maybe Samson got him."

"So it's a bull."

"I never said that. I said—"

Mr. Gibbons interrupted me. "I heard what you said. How do you know the calf's a bull? You know the value of a good bull."

I felt low-down lying to Mr. Gibbons about Ruby. I couldn't look at him anymore. I sure couldn't tell him Ruby was inside on my bed again. Instead I eyed his banged up truck outside the barn door, the same truck he drove up in that summer he came to build my treehouse. Mr. Gibbons never changed nothing.

When I was five, Mr. Gibbon's pick-up, old even then, rattled across the cattle grate on a yellow Saturday morning. I dashed to the porch, letting the screen door slam. Poking out of the truck bed were boards, wide and long. I ran to meet Mr. Gibbons. He lifted me high and flew me in circles above his head.

"Today's the day," he called out. "We're making you a fine treehouse."

"Where?"

"Right here in this old chinaberry tree. It's done it's growing and ready to have a little girl's treehouse sitting on this lowest branch."

I shouted for M'dear to come see.

By early afternoon, the treehouse sat on a sturdy limb that branched out from the trunk at a true forty-five-degree angle. It was complete with four-foot walls, a solid floor, a ladder that led up three-feet off the ground and a roof that slanted against the sun. I pulled the sheet off my bed and, trailing it in the dirt, ran for the ladder. I stuffed the sheet into a far corner and sat. I was a queen on her throne. This would be perfect for spying.

M'dear stepped up high enough to peep in. "Well," she said. "Your own private hidey-hole."

With M'dear's feet back on the ground, Mr. Gibbons climbed up. "You got your own play-house now. Every little girl needs a playhouse, I reckon."

"Thank Mr. Gibbons, Margaret Ann." M'dear bent her face toward Mr. Gibbons. "You too good to us, Mr. Gibbons."

Mr. Gibbons shook his head. "Just helping out some."

"Thank you, Mr. Gibbons." I hope he heard the glad in my voice.

Mr. Gibbons winked at me. I giggled.

"Remember my treehouse, Mr. Gibbons?"

"Yep. You getting 'bout too big for that little room."

"No. I won't ever leave it. It's my true spe-cial place." I patted Hazel's nose as she chewed. "That's the truth." I could go from my room and sit in the front corner of the treehouse and hear everything said on the porch. I kept a bucket of

187

dried chinaberries there with a big needle and thread for stringing necklaces and bracelets.

"Do you think you'll ever have a little girl like me?" I rubbed the toe of my shoe into the hay.

"Oh, I'm too old for having a kid." He took off his cap and slapped his thigh. "Guess you'll have to do."

"But what if I disappoint you?" It was hard to say that, but I had lied to him, in a way. "I know M'dear's disappointed that I'm not going back to the clinic."

"'Phelia ain't disappointed. She wants what's best for you, but you don't need to be going back there. Not never. You need to stay here and get them sores well." He patted me on my head and ran his hand down Hazel's spine. "You girls see that nothing happens to that young bull."

"Yes, sir," I said. I could've swore he sniggered as he left the barn.

I stepped over Baa when I came into the kitchen. M'dear never looked my way. Instead, she bent over the stove and took in the smell of fresh peas as their rawness boiled out.

"I ain't going back." I said it out loud to make M'dear know it was true. "I know you want me to because you think it's what's best, but I ain't going back. I might not even ever go back to that old colored school."

"Humph." Ophelia doused Blues' white cotton shirt with fresh water.

When M'dear didn't say nothing, I said more. "No use begging. I'm twelve. Can decide for myself." I opened the refrigerator door and let the cool air brush over me. Not seeing what I wanted—I didn't know what I wanted—I slammed the door. The tin breadbox on the top rattled.

"My. Oh my. Oh my," M'dear groaned.

I smelled the burnt cloth across the room. "You ruint that shirt." I never knew M'dear to burn somebody else's clothes. "What you going to do now?"

"We doing what's best. Pain or no pain."

"What you mean–pain or no pain?"

M'dear threw the shirt in a pan and poured water on it for cooling. Brown cloth dissolved, leaving behind the perfect shape of the iron. She bent over the sink. Her tears dropped on the damaged shirt.

"M'dear?"

"Go on 'bout your business now." M'dear straightened her back. She pulled up her skirt exposing her thighs and wiped her face. "Some things got to be done."

I had never seen so much of my mother's exposed skin. She was perfect, more beautiful than I had imagined. I ducked my head. There on the floor lay Baa. I picked him up and rubbed his naked cloth across my cheek. I went into my bedroom and sprawled across the bed on my stomach.

Through my thinking, I settled on the truth. If I was Hazel's mother, I would let Mr. Gibbons keep giving her shots. She needed to be strong, even though I know how much those shots hurt. Would I tell Mr. Gibbons "Don't give her no more shots cause she bawls when you do?" If Hazel got foot rot and fever and couldn't walk, would I say to Mr. Gibbons he can't give her penicillin shots to make her better? She's my baby—her and Ruby. I can't let them suffer when it could be stopped. I'm M'dear's baby. She must be thinking the same thing.

I went into the kitchen. M'dear sat at the table, her iron unplugged.

"We'll make it right by Brother Blues," I said. "We can give him a couple of laying hens for the shirt."

M'dear sniffed.

"I been thinking I might need go back to the clinic. I can take the sores alright, but I don't know I'll go back to school." I sat across from M'dear and waited for her to answer.

"You'll go back to school. If I have to see the principal or Eb Hawkins myself. Maybe go see them both. Get on to bed now. We'll catch us some hens in the morning."

I settled myself as best I could on my bed. Later in the night, I heard sounds from M'dear's room. I climbed out my window and followed a thick chinaberry limb so I could see what M'dear was doing. There she was, kneeling by her bed, her hands clasped together. She had thrown her head back, and tears wet her cheeks. She was mumbling something. I listened harder. Then I couldn't listen no more. I crept back to my bed. My M'dear was in the next room praying over me. I wanted to run and scream or beat my head against the wall for causing her so much pain.

Chapter 24

Tuesday morning, I went back to school, just like M'dear told me. The bell sounded, ending the first class, and I came out the cooking room door. A shuffling of feet sounded from under the stairwell. I spied Nell's gang sticking their faces out. Everybody but Patsy Green and Nell. I walked by on the other side of the hall. Patsy stepped out of the crowd. She grabbed my hair. I squealed against the pull. Nell whipped out her brother's knife, its blade bright as brand-new.

I twisted away, tying my hair into a loop. "Stop it!" I screamed.

Patsy yanked my head back, exposing my neck. "Cut her," she hissed to Nell. "Cut her."

Nell Hawkins never said a word. Thinking back on that now, I take in how disturbing that was.

Students scattered. Patsy Green yanked again and whispered in my ear, "You ought to kill yourself so we won't have to." I screamed again. From the woodworking shop, Bailey Renfroe run down the hall, yelling, "Leave her be." Two more steps and he pushed Patsy. Patsy let my hair go free. Nell gave the knife a wide swath. It swished as it passed me.

Bailey Renfroe clutched his arm and fell to the floor, blood spurting through his fingers. I dropped next to him. His eyes were closed. The long blade had sliced through Bailey Renfroe's shirt and into his upper arm.

The janitor Ole Zeke Pinion appeared out of the mess and bent over Bailey. "Why you do this to this boy?" He glared at me. He must have thought I had cut my best friend.

I froze and stared at the old man. I made no attempt to get up. Bailey Renfroe's blood felt warm as it seeped into my skirt and against my leg. It pinned me to the floor.

"Answer me, girl," Ole Zeke Pinion said. He turned toward the cooking room door and shouted, "Get out here and help me 'fore this boy, he die."

Two teachers dashed out. "I'm getting the principal," yelled the woodworking teacher on the run. Mrs. Garret gagged at the sight of Bailey Renfroe in all his blood and rushed to the garbage can. I heard her vomit hit the tin bottom.

"Have mercy," said Ole Zeke Pinion, shaking his white head. "More to clean up."

I sat on the floor, sobbing. "It was me. It weren't meant to be Bailey." I buried my face in my arms. "Not Bailey Renfroe."

"I reckon so," moaned Ole Zeke Pinion. No sound came from the kids who stood gawking on the other side of the hall.

Principal Wilson appeared. "Get out the way." Principal tore off his fine white shirt and wrapped Bailey's arm around and around. Blood soaked through as fast as he wrapped. More blood ran from his chest to his waist.

I couldn't take my eyes off all the blood. My hands trembled. I tapped my finger into the puddle that had formed by my knees. The blood spoke to me. "*Taste me,*" it said. I jerked my finger back and wiped it on my blouse. Bailey Renfroe's blood left a black stain against the pale cotton. The blood had emptied so fast he would bleed to death before they could get him to the colored doctor on the other side of Prattville. It had to be miles away. The principal lifted Bailey Renfroe in his arms and ran for the open double doors.

"Get up." Ole Zeke Pinion tugged my arm. "Get up and get yourself on home 'fore you cause more trouble." He moved around to lift me from the back. "You ain't got no cause to be spreading your dog days' sores around here." He tugged at my weight. "And now this, too."

I felt my jaw. What I had thought was a pimple was now an open sore oozing a sticky liquid. I wiped my hand on my sleeve and felt a sore on my upper arm rupture under the cloth.

My legs wouldn't hold me up. I crawled in a circle like a pup and lifted myself with my hands. My skirt, wet with blood, stuck to my legs. I walked a wobbly line to the door following blood splatters all the way, down the steps and into the shade where Principal parked his ugly, pink Edsel. The car was gone. Bailey Renfroe's blood disappeared in the dust.

Chapter 25

August was gone, and September had come in like summer's twin. Miss Claire knocked on the door at ten o'clock. It was Sunday, the first day of September. I had survived six weeks of shots. Bailey Renfroe lay in some hospital bed over in Prattville.

"I'm taking your invitation to go hear Brother Blues. I know he won't begin until 3:00, but I wanted to see about Margaret Ann. Can I come in?"

M'dear opened the screen without a word. Miss Claire sat at the kitchen table with M'dear and me. She had on a yellow dress with big red roses and a thin strap across each shoulder and yellow sandals from the day of the wreck. I tried to decide if I needed to tell her that her sundress might not please the matrons. Neither would her straw hat with fat red roses around the brim. I didn't say nothing. I'd look funny enough myself wearing bandages to hide the sores on my arms.

I spoke first. "You hear about Bailey Renfroe and what ol' Nell Hawkins done to him?"

"I did. I came by Brother Blues' store yesterday. When Bailey wasn't there, Brother Blues told me he was still in the hospital in Prattville."

"That Nell Hawkins, she's crazy." I bit my lip to stop the quiver. "M'dear burned my dress in the trash."

"Couldn't tolerate it bleeding all that little boy's blood in my wash machine." M'dear hung her head.

"About church. Or preaching. Can I go with you? I brought Daddy's old farm truck. It's rickety, but it'll be better than walking in this heat."

"You want to hear Blues?" M'dear said. "Why?"

"I don't know. I've argued with myself all week—to go or not to go. Never been a churchgoer, but this morning I woke up needing to hear what he has to say.

My mother sees only black or white. It's harder and harder to live with her. I need to see both, if I plan to stay around here. Maybe it comes from the feelings I get when I see Margaret Ann waiting as I drive over the cattleguard. Standing there glowing with so much gentleness and innocence. I can't tolerate what's happening to you anymore, girl."

I felt the heat on my face. I didn't answer. I didn't know what to say.

"Something's been drawing me to your preacher since Friday of the wreck. Maybe it's his difference. He's so deep a brown he could hide himself in shadows if he wants. But he doesn't try to hide. He stands tall and straight, but it's more than that. Blues Marshall has words I need to hear. He knows things about the world that I need to know.

He speaks the truth. No one has told me that. I sense it when I'm near him. Not because he's laid his hand on the Bible and labeled himself 'preacher,' but 'cause he has an aura of credibility I've never seen in another man. Walter Gibbons comes close to having that integrity." She put out her hand to me. "I've seen how he treats you, Margaret Ann. He's devoted to you. And to you, Miss Odom." Miss Claire waited like she had said too much. She stretched her neck and continued.

"I need to go to church. I'll sit apart so I won't be noticed. I can slip in late and leave early, if need be. When I took this job, I thought I knew what I was doing, but now, Margaret Ann, your health and personality have changed so. I'm afraid I've caused that."

"You welcome to go," said M'dear . "No need to set apart. Come sit by me here."

"Last night I recalled reading somewhere that there's a dark side of life." Miss Claire sat and spoke right at M'dear. "The writer compared our life source to a root that gets so tangled it kills itself. Eventually, the tangling kills whatever it touches, and then it self-destructs. That set me to wondering if perhaps, even though I'm White, that my life with my father grumbling about me and my job here – he's against the races mixing - and my mother kowtowing to him. My life might be the dark side, you know? Your life, yours and Blues Marshall's lives, Miss Ophelia, bring in the light.

So I want to go. Do I look alright, you think?"

"You fine," said M'dear And it was so.

Miss Claire and us parked on the side of the road in front of Brother Marshall's store. Three trucks had parked under the shade and a four-door sedan, dark green, blocking the three trucks from leaving. M'dear laughed a good belly laugh. "Some mama means for somebody to stay until the last 'Amen."

"I'm not sitting with you. I don't want to cause you trouble." Miss Claire walked through the store to the back door. It opened to a grassless spot under the massive live oak tree. M'dear and me walked around from the front of the store and took a seat at the back of the gathering.

Our congregation's mostly women who sit on overturned wooden boxes. A few bring their folding chairs, the seats and backs woven with candy colored plastic strips. Young kids chase each other across the next field in the way of chickens freed from their coop.

I watched Miss Claire take her place. She smoothed her dress over her hips and lowered herself to the floor in the back doorway. She dropped her feet on the rock step. She couldn't see me or M'dear, but I could see her real good. So could Brother Blues.

He pulled a spindly metal rack across the ground, the one that held boxes of peanut butter crackers and Little Debbies in the store. It left four shallow ruts in the dirt. He up-righted it in front of the people and placed his Bible, opened to a marked page, on the top shelf. A hot breeze blew the tissue-thin pages over and lost his place. Rather than thumb through to find it, he closed the book.

"Children of God." He spoke so quiet I strained to hear. "Let's go to the Lord." All heads turned to our preacher.

He raised both hands, palms toward the sky, and began to hum, his eyes closed. Others picked up the tune and from near the back row came the strong sound of an alto. *Walk in the light. Beautiful light.* Miss Claire stretched her neck to see where the voice came from. An older matron dressed in a spotless white suit sang with her hands raised as if reaching for highest branches of the oak. As she sang, more joined in, one or two at a time, until everybody sang in unison. *Weary souls, be restored.* The music echoed off the building and settled across the road in the cattle pasture.

The song ended like it started – sudden.

Preacher clasped his metal rack and said, "We all here this afternoon. God, He be here this afternoon."

A few eyes shifted in Miss Claire's direction. She folded her hands in her lap. I could tell she was embarrassed by her naked shoulders. The thin spaghetti straps made her look like a floozy. She pulled her sun hat down to hide her eyes and tried to cover herself with her arms. I should've told her. I let her down, I was letting everybody who cares about me down.

"You here now so we's can have some church." He lifted his Bible in his left hand and held it like a beacon. "Let's have some church." His voice rose higher and higher until he shouted out "Amen," like he was announcing a long-sought victory. Answers from several voices chanted "Amen," "Yes, Lord. Amen," and a man stood, his overalls starched stiff as what Preacher wore, rose and called out, "Be with us here this day, Precious Jesus."

The heat was unbearable, but each woman wore long sleeves and stockings. The men had their white Sunday shirts buttoned up to their chins, sleeves buttoned at their wrists. Women pressed thin handkerchiefs with tatted edges to their cheeks, the napes of their necks. Men removed their felt hats and fanned their faces. I saw Miss Claire's sweat run down her temples and drip into her ears, but she didn't move.

Out of the silence, came Preacher's voice again. "Ole Moses, he know where to go. He know that wicked White pharaoh be sitting up there on a hill daring them slaves to drop that shiny brass knocker on his door."

Women nodded their heads. Men stomped their feet, stirring up a fog of dust around their work shoes. Several chuckled at the scene Preacher painted.

"They tells you it be for your own good. Just like the massas a hundred years ago say being a slave is better than being free and lost." Preacher wiped his brow. "But we ain't lost, Brothers and Sisters. We ain't lost."

A chorus of agreement soared over the crowd.

Preacher's voice rose. "Where are we, people of Hyssop, Alabama? I tell you. We stands in the shadow of a White pharaoh, same as Moses. He don't live on no hill. No. He live on a knoll over by Hyssop and gathers his peoples around his feet to do his will." Preacher spoke quiet-like, as if he was sharing a secret. "They's evil in this land. Ole Moses, he saw the evil. He saw the way out and led his people home."

At this point, Miss Claire removed her hat. She used it to fan her face. M'dear tapped my leg. "Pay attention, Margaret Ann," she murmured as she beamed at Preacher.

"Moses, ole faithful Moses, he asked God to show a sign and God, He did. Signs of frogs." The congregation agreed. "Yes."

"Signs of flies."

"Yes."

"And dead cattles," shouted Preacher.

Miss Claire mouthed her own "Yes."

"And when that evil pharaoh he couldn't see the signs, God, He sent his Angel of Death to strike down the first born. Even the pharaoh's first born," Preacher spoke above a whisper.

The congregation nodded and sounded hum-hums. The matron in white called out "Lord have mercy. Mercy."

Preacher continued. "We's got signs here in Hyssop. Yes, indeed. We got drought." He looked toward the sky as if he expected rain to fall. When none did, he continued. "A long, long drought."

The congregation agreed.

"We got our childrens breaking out in boils. Boils, I tell you."

He's talking 'bout me, I thought. I looked to M'dear . She shook her head.

The matrons of the congregation looked at each other as if somebody would identify the guilty. I crossed my arms and put my hands over my bandages.

"These our childrens. These babes ain't evil. No, Lord. These childrens is being set upon by demons. Demons in a White man's clothes. First one. And now three more. We got childrens who wants to leave this earth behind cause of the pain Satan is putting on their bodies."

Preacher quieted his voice again. "We's one people."

The people hummed in agreement. Miss Claire nodded.

"We's going to be free of this demon, like Moses freed his people out of Egypt." Preacher waited for a response. "But we's going, people. We is going."

"Amens" answered throughout the congregation.

"Now. We's being cursed. Cursed, I say." He waited for his words to sink in. "The first born is being taken."

People looked at each other, trying to know this mystery.

"Thursday, this past Thursday, Sister Bella Whitstone's girl, she went to the Free Women's Clinic. When she come out, Miss Claire sitting there in the door can witness for her. Saw her dropping blood on the floor and offered to help her."

Miss Claire flinched and grabbed her throat. I thought she was about to jump and run when Preacher called her name.

"But we know Sister Bella and her independence and that wicked man of hers. Late in the night, something broke loose and that girl died in her own bed. Bled to death, she did."

Gasps sounded like a working beehive.

"Sister Bella ask that we help her lay her girl by next Sunday. We be here for her and stay with her until we learn what happened to one of our own. Stay with me, my people."

Preacher hummed again. Others picked up

the melody line. Within a moment, the alto matron broke out the words *Precious Lord, take my hand. Lead me on, let me stand.* Miss Claire rose and walked to the woman. The woman stood and looked at Miss Claire without missing a note.

Miss Claire placed her arm around the singer's shoulders. She dropped her hat to the ground and laid her head against the woman's afro. I watched, my mouth hanging open. They sang together, alto and soprano, voices blending as if the two was family who had sung their lives through. The congregation lifted their hands heavenward. At the end of the song, the woman wiped tears from her eyes.

Miss Claire dabbed at her eyes and stepped away. She picked up her hat and walked to the back door of the store. Behind her, Preacher had sung out his sermon. And all God's people said, "Amen."

"Amen," Brother Blues said.

Chapter 26

Miss Claire stopped at the steps leading into the back of the store and waved a tiny wave to me. I lifted my hand to say goodbye. Members stood around in little groups talking low—probably about Miss Claire being there and singing out loud. Me and M'dear walked up to Brother Blues.

"How's Bailey Renfroe?" I asked.

"Seems to be doing a mite better this morning. If he weren't, I wouldn't be here today. Come to love that boy hard."

"When's he coming home from the hospital? I can bring his homework."

"They ain't saying just yet. Kind of you, Margaret Ann. He thinks a whole lot of you, you know." In a blink, Brother Blues' face went lifeless.

I glimpsed where he was looking and caught my breath.

A leggy policeman from the county sheriff's office had appeared around the corner, his blue uniform wet under the arms from the heat. He settled his gun toward the front of his hip. Everybody shushed. Every eye sized him up and down. I whispered to M'dear, "What's a White policeman doing here?" She clamped her hand over my mouth.

The policeman spread his legs like he thought he was some grand statue. He pushed his hat up on his head with his finger. "Zeke Pinion here?" His voice traveled over the congregation and fluttered out into the field. I looked across the road to see if Hazel was there, but she was a good mother. She would be safe in her stall with Ruby.

A second policeman stepped from the front of the store. He guzzled a coca-cola and chewed on peanuts he had poured into the bottle. Chewing with his gums showing, he grinned with his mouth, but not his eyes.

Old Zeke Pinion stood. "I be's Ezekiel Pinion." He drug his name out long and slow. Then added "Sir." Nobody but me watched Old Zeke.

"Come with me, boy, and there won't be trouble."

"What I done?"

"We'll see. We need you to answer some questions over in Sweetwater."

"'Bout what?" Old Zeke hadn't moved a step.

"Knifing over at that colored school Tuesday. I hear you was there."

"Yes, sir, I was." His forehead sweated, but he never lifted the crumpled handkerchief in his fist.

"We need to hear about it. Over in Sweetwater. Let's not make trouble."

"Why you not asking the knifer, that Hawkins girl? I ain't knifed nobody."

"Can't find her. Her and that Patsy Green run off in the night. So Eb says. Took the knife but left that boy of hers." Sweat dripped from under his policeman's cap.

"I tell you what happened without going to Sweetwater. She swung at that high yeller gal over there." He nodded toward me. I shriveled inside. "Missed and cut the Renfroe kid. That's all. I cleaned up the blood and emptied the can where the cooking teacher puked. That's all."

"Well, that's not all exactly. See, that Renfroe boy done died about half a hour ago over in the colored ward at Prattville. So we ain't talking a knifing no more. We talking killing."

Brother Blues bent at the waist and howled a animal scream that I never want to hear ever again. He dropped his Bible, and a little puff of dust lifted and settled on the leather backing.

I wailed. M'dear hugged me face-first to her bosom. I screamed more and some more. I tried to scream it out of my brain. Not Bailey Renfroe. Not my friend. Not Bailey Renfroe who tried to protect me. Patsy's words came back in my mind. "You ought to kill yourself so we won't have to." Now they had killed my best friend instead of me.

I couldn't keep it in. I wanted to run, but M'dear held me too tight. I tried to drop to the ground, but M'dear held me up. I wanted to die, but M'dear squeezed my back and my breath kept coming and coming. What am I going to do without Bailey Renfroe? I held my breath so I could die, but I got dizzier and dizzier.

From far away, came Bailey Renfroe's voice as clear as the day I ran away in the fields. "Look for me in the dust," it had said.

"It's the dust." Panic locked my knees stiff. I felt myself falling. Then floating. The whole place turned black before I hit the ground.

Chapter 27

When I woke the next morning, nothing in the dark looked familiar. A shaft of light cut across the floor. In a dim corner stood three people, backs turned, heads bent. Mr. Gibbons had his arm around M'dear's shoulder and his head against hers. I could tell she was crying by the way her shoulders heaved. Brother Blues was nowhere around. Then I remembered that Bailey Renfroe was killed. I couldn't breathe. It held until I choked. Brother Blues would've gone to Prattville to be a sort-of-daddy to Bailey. I hoped the people there wouldn't give him a hard time getting Bailey Renfroe back.

I pulled back the sheet on the sofa and tried to sit up, but the pain in my hips stopped me. M'dear must have heard me stir. She came and leaned over me. Her face wet from crying. Mr. Gibbons and Miss Claire laughed a funny little laugh and hugged like family.

"Don't cry, M'dear. It's okay." But she couldn't stop. Not for a minute. Mr. Gibbons put his hands under her arms and lifted her. She turned and bawled into his shirt. "It's my fault. I done this," she kept saying over and over. Mr. Gibbons shushed her and Miss Claire patted her back.

"If it's somebody's fault, it's mine, Miss Ophelia." Miss Claire claimed her due. She wore her sadness with great regret. Mr. Gibbons shook his head as if telling her to hush.

I couldn't take it anymore. "Shut up. It's mine to own. Should've been me cut. She aimed for me. I dodged and Bailey Renfroe took the blade." My pulse throbbed in my head. "I'm the blame. I should've been dead. I killed Bailey Renfroe, as sure as I pulled the knife myself."

The silence in the room was so strong I could hear people breathing. I should swipe all three of them down and get to Prattville to help Brother Blues. "I'm going to Prattville." I sat up despite the throb in my hip.

Mr. Gibbons gripped my arms. I yelped, but he held me fast. "Sit down. You ain't going nowhere but to your bed. Come along now, like a good girl." M'dear slid to the floor.

I could feel the blood's rhythm in my head, it hurt so bad. I squeezed my forehead. "M'dear?" I said. "Come and lie with me."

"I'll get her a dose of paregoric," said Miss Claire.

The medicine tasted better than candy. I took the bottle and drank a long drink. Miss Claire snatched the bottle from my hands and barked at me "You trying to kill yourself?"

Mr. Gibbons took the bottle, and I didn't see it again.

"M'dear?" She led me to my bed. I curled as close as I could be to M'dear and fell asleep.

The dream was so real, I still couldn't believe it was a dream. In the dream, me and Bailey Renfroe climb out my window on the big limb of my chinaberry tree. I clamber to the next limb and hoist Bailey Renfroe up next to me. Then to the next. We got a method. I go up. I lift Bailey up. And on we go until we reach the highest limb, so high we could soar. We sit side by side. My real mind tells me none of this is true cause I could never lift Bailey up nowhere, he's so round. But here we are. We can't climb no more. We gaze out over the pasture and watch the cattle gloat on new grass, grass so tall you can't see their knees. So quiet. No sound — not even the birds.

In the distance, hyssop is blooming like crazy. Purple as far as we can see. We don't talk. We just watch. Hazel wanders by. Ruby follows her like a puppy. Ruby is a puppy. The little brown puppy Samson had killed early summer. Hazel concentrates on her way. She makes a new path through the grass to the cattle pond. Long grass bends as Hazel passes through, and then closes behind her. Ruby holds her head high to see where her mother's going.

In the far end of the pond, white water bubbles up from the spring to make fresh water and push out the stale. Hazel goes into the pond without a stumble or slide and stands in the center up to her belly. She don't move. She's a black statue wearing a policeman's blue hat. Ripples move in slow, slow motion, one following the other. Ruby tries to reach Hazel, but her legs are short and her hooves are tiny. She slips and goes down. She busts back up and shakes water off her head.

From where we sit, we see water sparkles on her back. Her shimmer disappears as she goes deeper, mimicking her mother. Hazel hasn't moved.

I want to yell to Ruby to come back. Only her head shows above the water. But she dog- paddles on, trying to reach her mother. "*Hazel*" my mind wants to cry, but when I open my mouth my jaws lock and I can't warn either of them. "*Don't lose your baby,*" my mind says, but I'm so far away, even if I called out, Hazel wouldn't hear me.

I cry. Big heavy tears wet my cheeks. Bailey Renfroe wipes them away and dries his hands on my shirt. He smiles a strange I'm-sorry-kinda smile, and I smile back. We climbed as high as we could. Bailey Renfroe and me. Our only choice now is to go down. I know Bailey Renfroe's heart. Like me, he's happy to stay up here.

A breeze rises. It stirs the leaves and chinaberries drop plop-plop to the ground. I recall the martins who got so drunk on the berries in July. I hear a tweet, but there's no birds. It's Bailey Renfroe. He's got a orange beak. Purple feathers sprout from the cuts on his arm and chest. He lifts the arm to fly, but he's too heavy to carry himself. He pumps his feathered wing again. I grab his other arm to hold him close. He jerks away and plunges to the ground. I can't scream. His splat wakes me.

I open my eyes. M'dear was gone from my bed.

Chapter 28

After my trip to the pharmacy in Montgomery and learning what had been done to Margaret Ann, I set out to do what I felt called to do. By early afternoon, I was back at the clinic. I stretched to relax, rolled a sheet of paper into the typewriter, and reflected on the bread vanishing into the toaster the other day. It had burned, and my mother had started over as if nothing had happened. But something had happened. Something was happening throughout Sweetwater. No one seemed willing to say something. I rolled the paper up the typewriter cartridge and typed. I reread what I had typed and signed my name. If any heat rose from my action, I would take it.

Two months had taught me more than I wanted to know. I had brought Margaret Ann physical and emotional harm. This day, September 2,

1968, would mark the day I took a stand against what was happening at the Free Women's Clinic.

I folded my letter of resignation and slipped it into one of the clinic's business envelopes. One swipe of my tongue, and it was sealed. No patients waited to see Dr. Graves, so I tapped on the examination room door. There was no answer. I walked down the hall back toward the lobby and knocked on the treatment room door. I breathed deep and waited. Nurse and Dr. Graves were in one of the two rooms. They had not left. There was no way out of the building other than through my line of vision.

I lifted my fist to knock again. The door opened, and there stood Dr. Graves, a stethoscope hanging around his neck. His crumpled medical jacket covered a white shirt and gray trousers. His tie's knot hung loose. Nurse stepped through the side door into the Examination Room, her face hidden behind a surgical mask. A strange musky odor burned my nose.

Dr. Graves's severe expression told me that only a tenuous thread held me to this job. But I was willing to cut that thread. Knowing that this stranger held such power over me made my hand tremble. "I won't cry. I won't," I said without thinking. I swallowed hard. "Not in front of you."

"My dear lady, why would I make you cry?" Dr. Graves slapped his thigh.

I offered the envelope. "Mr. Bullard said I am to report to you and only you. This is my resignation." When Graves didn't take the envelope, I dropped my hand. "I can't work here anymore." My determination withered with an intense need to explain. Explaining would not change what had happened to Margaret Ann. The realization that this man had proven himself no better than a low-down hound bolstered my determination. I put the envelope before him again.

"Come inside and let's talk this out," said Dr. Graves. He ignored the envelope. He took my elbow and steered me toward a metal chair.

I drew back. "There's nothing to talk out. I'm quitting. That's all."

Dr. Graves reached again for my arm.

A physical confrontation had never entered my mind. I whirled around and stomped toward the door.

"You can't quit. You know that, don't you?"

"Of course I can quit. You can't hold me here."

Dr. Graves turned the bolt on the door. With the sound of the metal click, my legs went limp. "Now, Miss Whitehurst. Claire, isn't it?" Dr. Graves pushed the chair toward me and swept his hand out, enticing me to sit. I couldn't move. "You don't want to leave such a lucrative job. All you do is keep records of who comes and who goes. You sometimes go out to the boonies." He corrected himself. "To outlying areas, let's say, and bring patients in and take them home. That's hardly a taxing job for the pay you receive."

He stepped closer. "You recall the commitment you made with Mr. Bullard, surely." I pulled in my arms. He would not touch me again. He moved closer. "An oral contract is as binding as a written one, you know. Walk out now and he'll keep his word. You won't work in this state again."

I had to concentrate to comprehend what he said. I had not expected to be locked inside the treatment room. "You need to open that door," I demanded. Moisture dampened the sleeves under my arms.

"Not until we talk about why you want to leave." Dr. Graves had edged between me and the door.

"Look, Dr. Graves," I said. I wiped sweat from my temple and looped my hair behind my ear. His brusque tone had made my voice terse. "You don't scare me." I glanced around for a way to walk around him toward a door. "I'm not working here anymore. I don't have to give you a reason. I just quit." I sidled closer to the door. Light entered through a crack from the adjoining room. "You can tell Nurse." I took another step. "Or I'll tell her so she won't have to eavesdrop behind this door."

Thinking I was quick, I reached for the doorknob. The examination room door slammed. Another click. Another lock. I glared at Dr. Graves. "What are you hiding here? Other than the fact that you and Nurse play doctor every day." My voice rose. "I know what you've been doing to these girls." I rattled the doorknob. "Let me out of here, Nurse. Right now."

The door opened as if I had turned the knob myself. Nurse stood in the door, still wearing her mask. She moved before I realized what she was doing. A sharp burn spread through my hip. I tried to walk, but I folded to the floor instead. My breath came in short, shallow spurts. The thought that I was going crazy bumped across my mind. I could not move. All I could see were two pairs of shoes—one pair dull, scuffed white and one brown Italian loafers—then nothing.

When I recovered, darkness filled the clinic. I groped around and turned on the overhead light. Nurse and Dr. Graves were gone. Medical supplies were missing. Cabinets were empty. Broken syringes and vials lay scattered over the floor. The door to the lobby stood ajar. I made my way out, dragging my left leg. File cabinet drawers hung open. All the records had disappeared.

I hobbled outside. I cranked the old Studebaker truck and drove without thought to the road. At the intersection, I had to turn—right for Prattville and home or left for Hyssop. The throb in my right hip told me which way to go. As I drove, a crescent moon offered only a slice of light. At Blues' store, all lights were out, the front door closed. I drove on.

Chapter 29

The truck bumped over the cattleguard. Each jolt aggravated my hip pain. I stopped in front of the thin metal gate that kept the black angus out of Ophelia's yard and turned off the headlights. A light came on in the back of the house, and the outline of Ophelia appeared at the screen.

I limped up the steps to the porch and reached for the screen door's handle only to find that Ophelia held it closed. I stared at my feet, remembering the first time I had appeared at this door.

"Miss Odom. I'm so sorry." I wrung my hands. "Miss Ophelia. I had no idea." I couldn't look at her face. "I never would have done anything like this to Margaret Ann."

"What you want?" Ophelia stood with splayed legs, firm, unmoving.

"I don't know." I hiccupped. "I need to make it right, and I don't know how." My crying amplified into shacking sobs.

"Hush." Ophelia whispered. "I don't want you waking Margaret Ann." Ophelia released her hold on the door. "Come in here and set a spell." She pushed the door out so I could enter.

I shuffled through the living room and sat in a chair at the kitchen table. So this was Margaret Ann and Ophelia's life. A plug adapter had been screwed between the socket and the light bulb hanging from the ceiling. A thin brown extension cord ran from one outlet to a cup hook in the ceiling and dropped to the floor where the iron's cord lay plugged in. Ophelia's ironing board stood by the one window, allowing her a view of the massive chinaberry tree that fed the martins Margaret Ann once told me about. I had never noticed the tree. Each time I arrived, I had focused on the front door and seeing Margaret Ann. A small box refrigerator sat in the far corner. An oilcloth covered the square table. It was so new its chemical smell filled the room. I followed a meandering ivy pattern with my index finger. My head felt so heavy I couldn't lift it.

Ophelia took a chair across from where I sat. "Why you here, Miss Whitehurst?" She flattened both hands on the table and appeared to study them.

"I know what they did and how they did it. She can't go back." I slid back in my chair and lifted my hip.

"Since when do you know so much and says nothing?" Ophelia gripped the edge of the table.

"I went to a pharmacist in Montgomery. They are giving her experimental drugs and her just a child." I leaned forward. Maybe closeness would make my story more believable.

"Humph."

"They're using the colored girls because they are colored. I think they might even be using surgery to sterilize them. I saw. . ." I didn't finish. I had no proof.

Ophelia pushed the saltshaker back and forth across the table. Tears wet her cheeks. She made no move to catch them.

"Hitler," I said. "It's just like what Hitler did to anybody he thought was unfit." I waited for Ophelia to chastise me. "I'm sorry. I promised to help Margaret Ann. I've done nothing but hurt her."

"Trying to do what's right ain't easy, Miss Whitehurst. Sometimes it's easier to do what's wrong and not worry about it."

"Nurse gave me a shot. It must have been morphine, because I couldn't breathe right. It knocked me out, and now they're gone with the records."

"Here. Drink this." Ophelia set a glass of water on the table. "Ain't got much, but I can fry you some eggs."

I shook my head. I wasn't hungry.

"One day, rain's coming," Ophelia said. "Don't know when, but it's coming."

I drank. "Rain?"

"Rain. It's coming." Ophelia rubbed her palm over the oilcloth. "Ain't the end of the world." Outside the window, a calf bawled.

"What's that?" I pulled my upper lip into my mouth and chewed.

"Ruby, that's all. She all right. Fussing 'cause your lights, they woke her up." Ophelia swatted her hand at a fly. "Figured Margaret Ann would've told you 'bout her and her cut leg. Her pet calf. Tried to hide her in her treehouse so Mr. Gibbons won't put her down." She laughed. "Silly kids. Her and Bailey Renfroe. Calf'll be fine soon as she heals. Pretty soon now, I reckon." Ophelia fanned at the fly again. "She in the barn. In Hazel's stall."

I rose to look out the window. I had an unexplained need to know everything about this child.

"Can't see him. Margaret Ann and Bailey Renfroe hid him good."

"Can I see Margaret Ann?" I stared out the window at the dark.

"If we be quiet. She's sleeping. This a bad, bad day." Ophelia shook her head as she spoke, but she rose and walked noiselessly into the next room.

Outside, the earth refused to cool. Ripples of heat rose from the ground and set shadows to wavering. No leaf rustled on the chinaberry tree.

"Come." Ophelia sat facing the window.

I walked across the kitchen and looked out at the chinaberry tree. "Those open places on Margaret Ann's chin?"

"Dog Days. Dog Days, they make sores be bad. Real bad. That's all." Ophelia pulled down a cluster of dried stems from the window sash and tossed them into the sink.

"They look like impetigo. I had it when I was little. It's really contagious." I took a chair from under the table and sat again. "Do other kids at school have them?"

"Don't know. Thought it most probably 'Blue Jennies' like she say. Nothing gone right since that clinic come to town. Arms and hip, too, but they ain't this bad." Ophelia rubbed her forehead. "These ones acting like they want to be scars. Right there on her pretty face."

Ophelia swayed as she spoke. "Her spirit had been ripped out by the likes of that Nell Hawkins and her cutting Bailey Renfroe and some nurse with no name. And now them blue jennies. All that was left was helplessness. Terrors to fill up the holes her spirit left." Ophelia nodded her head. "True enough. I know my baby girl."

I hesitated but placed my arm around Ophelia's shoulders. "What did you say?"

"I know my baby," Ophelia answered.

"No. About blue jennies. Margaret Ann mentioned blue jennies the day of the wreck." My hands shook. "She meant eugenics. She didn't know that word, so she thought she heard Blue Jennies." The reality of what Ophelia had said turned my voice squeaky. Margaret Ann tried to turn over but gave up as she moaned in the next room. Ophelia led me to the table where we could talk without whispering. She sat me in a straight-back chair. "Oh my god, Mrs. Odom. I could have killed her."

"What's this eugenics?"

"It's sterilization, making it impossible for a woman to have a child." My shoulders drooped. I wanted to vanish through the floor.

"My baby, no reason to want her to not to have no babies. She not old enough yet. She not even got her first full blood."

"The shots. They're experiments to see if they can keep her from having her first blood. They've been using her for research, for tests. They've been using all the girls I brought in there in some way or another."

"Nobody do that to her. She never hurt nobody. I ain't believing you." Ophelia looked into my eyes. Their bottomless brown seemed to reach into my deepest thoughts. "She born not long after that Till boy they beat up and lynched over in Money, Mississippi in '55. He fourteen." Ophelia pondered for a quiet time. "Maybe you right. Maybe they testing her 'cause she not White. They's more than one way to kill a child, Miss Whitehurst. More than one way."

I shook my head as if to clear my thoughts. I covered my mouth to hide a yawn. The shot. It was making me drowsy.

"Mightn't you need to take to bed for a while?" Ophelia offered. "Sleep on that couch there 'till morning? This heat don't call for no covers."

"You're offering a White woman a bed in your house?" So tired. I leaned toward Ophelia.

"In my house, ain't no White. Ain't no Black," Ophelia answered. "Don't say it out loud and it ain't so. Come on now. Rest."

"Better not. Only Mama knows I didn't go to work today." I covered another yawn. It was as if, once I cried myself out and relaxed at knowing Margaret Ann was safe in bed, my own energy had zapped away. "Best I go on."

Ophelia maintained eye contact. "I tell you this for true." Ophelia's eyes held me rooted. "The Reverend Mr. King, he say 'A time comes when silence is betrayal.' I ain't betraying my girl and, knowing you, you ain't neither. I ain't holding in no more."

I staggered toward the couch. "You need to know. I went to the paper before I quit this morning. Soon everybody'll know."

Ophelia broke into tears.

"Come tomorrow, I'll take her to Prattville or Montgomery. Get something for the sores. Make sure she's okay."

"No. Mr. Gibbons or Blues. They take us. You done enough."

I sat on the couch. "Yes, ma'am. I never meant to do wrong."

"Me neither," said Ophelia, more to herself than anyone else.

"Everything's getting crazy." What was left of the shot took effect again. I stretched out and slept.

"A sweeter thing God never made," I whispered as I stood over Margaret Ann's bed near the morning's light.

I heard a sob behind me and turned to see Ophelia, her face in her hands, crying. I went to her and placed my arms around her shoulders. Her tears wet my blouse. I led her out of the room and into the kitchen.

We sat at the table, as we had the last evening. "I got to send her north, Miss Whitehurst," Ophelia stammered out.

"Do you know somebody to send her to?" I clasped my hands over Ophelia's.

Ophelia nodded. "Blues, he got a sister in Ohio. Paulette. She take her in."

"Who told you to send her north?" I pressed my elbows on the table to steady my hands.

"I been thinking it all month." Ophelia swallowed hard. "She don't belong here, being mixed and all. Hyssop won't have her. Sweetwater won't have her. Her own daddy won't have her." Ophelia took the saltshaker and again pushed it back and forth across the table.

"I thought Mr. Gibbons brought money each month for her. That's what Margaret Ann told me. If Mr. Gibbons is willing to bring money for her, surely he'd claim her as his own. Even if all three of you have to move." I reached out a hand to take Ophelia's.

Ophelia jerked her hand back. "You thinking Margaret Ann . . .? Me and Mr. Gibbons . . .?" Ophelia laughed aloud. "Law me, chil'. If Walter Gibbons be her daddy, we be long gone from here."

Embarrassment shot up my neck and over my face.

"Walter Gibbons too good a man to throw away a child, no matter her color." Ophelia stared out the kitchen door. Outside a morning bird fussed about another day of boiling sun.

I spoke just above a whisper. "I'm sorry. I didn't mean to pry. Of course, not Mr. Gibbons. How can I be so dumb?"

"Girl, you listen to me," Ophelia looked eye to eye at me. "Cause a little brown snake look like a big fat worm don't mean he ain't still a snake. Snakes hide in the safest of places and strike you from far off. You ever see a copperhead in the woods?"

I shook my head.

"No, you ain't. That don't mean they ain't there. They there alright. They just looks like a stick or a oak limb, but you get too close they rise up and take you down."

"I don't understand what you're saying," I said.

"I'm saying Margaret Ann's daddy is a ful-ly-growed copperhead."

Chapter 30

From the open window, I heard voices, a man and a woman, trying to be quiet. I slipped out the window and shimmied down the big limb that supports my treehouse. In the square window and across the floor, I crouched in the corner so I could hear what they was talking about. Always my best spying plan. I peeped around the door opening and saw M'dear now sitting on the porch by herself. Mr. Gibbons came out carrying the blue speckled wash pan. The screen popped shut.

"Here, 'Phelia. Soak your feet in this cool water. Get some of that swelling down."

Mr. Gibbons sat in his usual spot on the porch with his back to the post. He gazed across the scorched pasture, without pinpointing any one spot. "We'll have a lot to remember, 'Phelia, once we leave this place."

"You leaving, Mr. Gibbons?" M'dear rubbed one foot over the other and dropped her back against her chair.

"Call me 'Walter,' 'Phelia. I mean, after all these years. All that's happened. Surely we know each other that well." He sniggered a little laugh up through his nose, the one he used when he figured I had hid Ruby from him. He paused to light his cigarette. "That night on the front porch when Margaret Ann played jacks and laughed when I beat her to grabbing that little red ball, I thought all was going okay. I thought you and her was safe."

"No Black woman's ever safe, Walter. Not nowhere. Not as long as people like Mr. Bullard come around."

"Something's going to be done about that. I can't talk it, but there's something. I know you don't think it's so lessen I say it out loud, but I can't. But I can say it's so. I don't want nobody hurt. But I don't want Margaret Ann's name drug through the mud like some slut neither. Nothing but a child. A child don't need no such gossip." He blew smoke toward the yard.

"For sure." M'dear stilled her feet and placed them flat against the bottom of the pan.

"You ever thought about leaving, 'Phelia?"

"Oh, sometimes. But where would I go? Leaving takes money. Once you get going, it takes having a place to stop. It takes more money once you get stopped from where you left. I ain't got neither." There was no complaining in her tone. She said it so matter-of-fact that her words caused Mr. Gibbons to look up at her.

"Boss never sent you enough money to lay some aside?"

M'dear didn't say.

"Of course, he wouldn't done that. He'd eat the damn money hisself before he'd give one dime to help somebody." He drew in more smoke. "I know that. What I don't know is why I keep working for him."

"You got your own obligations."

A puff of dust rose on the breeze. I would rather have a cool breath of air, but the air, though moving, was as hot as it had been all day. Both M'dear and Mr. Gibbons waited for the dust to drop before either spoke.

Mr. Gibbons lifted his right foot off the top step and set it by the left, as if he meant to get up. "What if I asked you to leave here? Leave with me?" Mr. Gibbons' voice plowed through the question as if it was soft ground, ready for planting. "Take Margaret Ann and go to California. People out there ain't so set in their ways."

"What you asking me, Walter Gibbons?" M'dear had yet to look at Mr. Gibbons.

"I reckon I'm asking you to run away. Put all this meanness behind us and go someplace where people're different." He thought for a minute. "Go with me and let us be a regular family. Get us some healing."

"Ain't no such place. Peoples always going to try to outdo peoples. Sometimes I think people just born mean. After Adam and that apple, ain't nobody worth killing."

With such a statement, I expected M'dear to rise from her chair to shake her fist at the heavens to stave off a lightning strike. I never heard her talk like that about nobody. Mr. Gibbons glimpsed back at her. At that point, M'dear could've declared her power, but she sat silent as a ghost.

I drew back into myself, like a snake ready to strike. I understood why she talked that way, what with my weeping sores, specially the one on my jaw, and Bella Whitstone's girl waiting to be buried, Nell Hawkins gone with her knife, and Bailey Renfroe maybe still over in Prattville being dead. Days wasn't looking too pleasing. I had a hard need to hug Hazel.

"I never knew you was so bitter, 'Phelia," Mr. Gibbons said.

"Me neither."

"Well, you think on it a spell." He stood, as if he planned to leave.

"I will, but I don't see much changing now." She slipped her feet into her broke down mules. "Not with my Sugar Baby hurting so. Her hurting's hurting me as much or more. Rather die than have my baby face more pain."

I clutched my throat. I knew M'dear was hurting, but not more than me. I hurt so bad I didn't want to go on. What kind of daughter was I? Killing my own M'dear .

"Got to find a trusty person 'fore I can step ahead," she said.

"I reckon so," Mr. Gibbons agreed. "That little girlie, she's too quiet. Won't say nothing. Stares off into space or she's squalling her head off. I understand why, but I don't understand how it come to be. She ain't the same little girl." He ground his cigarette into the dirt and turned toward the road. "Mull over it, if you're willing."

Mr. Gibbon's tires whomped as they crossed the cattle grate. Once the sound died, M'dear entered her house and closed the screen door for the night. I eased back into bed to think a bit.

I still cry when I'm by myself. I cried real hard that night. Now I knew what pain I was causing. When I quit, I prayed. I asked God to give me an easy death. I know it's coming. And I pray what I know. "Now I lay me down to sleep, and please do not wake me up in the morning."

Chapter 31

Outside the fence that surrounds our house and my chinaberry tree, there's a barn for the heifers who are dropping calves, which they seem to be doing all the time. Out from the barn is the cattle pond. It's a wondrous pond, always cool. So cool sometimes when the sun draws up the coolness, a feathery mist makes its way toward the sky. That pond saved the cattle during the summer of no rain. It could have saved me, if I had known how to die.

I thought in my mind about why I should or should not. I saw nothing ahead but emptiness. I didn't know why the darkness was there in my mind. But I felt my body being hollow. I feel it now. A coldness inside.

I'm sad, so very sad, now that Bailey Renfroe's gone. My head's so heavy. I don't care about nothing. Nothing at all. That night, I laid there thinking *I'm by myself now, and I'm not seeing a time when it'll be any other way.* You don't know about lonesome until nighttime quiet wakes you and you know you never know a person really. I thought I knew Bailey Renfroe, but probably not.

Before I left our house that night, I hugged M'dear hard. I wanted to tell her everything with that quiet hug, but I couldn't. I wanted to tell her that I understood that she was the best M'dear she knew how to be, since she'd not had nobody for her growing up. So what I meant to do didn't matter. I was stronger than I had been when I stood in front of the cattle truck. But I couldn't shake Patsy's words out of my mind. "You ought to kill yourself," she'd said. So much needed to be witnessed, but there wasn't nobody to listen except Bailey Renfroe and he was good and dead.

I talked to Bailey Renfroe about being so lonesome. "You don't know lonesome," I said. "You gone. I'm by myself. And I'm scared."

Out of nowhere, he told me, "Get over it, Odom. Lonesome is not like being dead where you don't ever get past it."

He was right, but it took me a long, long time to know that. The lonesome has lasted longer than it took for the sores to go away. A lot longer.

After a time, a light darkness came on. Over the rise that hid the cattle pond, I pushed my fear ahead of myself and followed it into the fresh spring water. It nourished Hazel. It could, in the contradictory way of water, pull out my breath and free me from the sadness that'd dogged me since I first went to the clinic.

Earlier, from behind the barn, I had collected rocks, round and smooth and long and sharp. I should've took sacks to fill. I didn't think of that, so I carried them in my hands. The dirt they'd collected over the drought ground into my palms. Sweat built up grit between my fingers. I wanted to wipe my hands against my gown, but I couldn't drop the rocks. I would need them when I got deep in the pond.

A full moon lit the land, made it easy to follow Hazel's path. Walking through the sedge in my white nightgown, I must have looked like some kind of spirit. The water, untouched from escaping underground, chilled my feet. Ripples caught the hem of my nightdress. Wetness slapped the thin cloth around my ankles. My skin tingled. My head pounded. The pain told me *this is the right thing*. Mud squished between my toes. I curled my toes into the bottom as I moved deeper into the water. As I pushed the water back toward the bank, my gown billowed out.

Near the middle of the pond, I lowered my hands to allow the rocks to pull me under. The weight only tired my sore arms. The mud was slick, slicker than near the bank. The rotten smell took me back to my runaway day and laying in the river water. My feet slid over the cushy bottom. I couldn't trust the mud to let me stand until I dropped the rocks, so I dropped them, one by one. At what I thought might be the center of the pond, water reached to my armpits. "M'dear'll be shamed that I cross the Jordan with unsoaped hands," I said out loud. But nobody heard me. Without another thought, I rubbed my hands together and over my body to cleanse me for Glory.

I sat. A swathe of water covered my head. My hair lifted and fanned out over the pond's surface. My mind's eye saw soft rushes ripped from the bottom. They rose and floated around me in a wide, black halo. My hair absorbed water, rather than beaded up when I'd oiled it, and I was glad. It floated out beautiful. I'm no longer ashamed that I got no kinks. I opened my mouth and took a deep swallow. Water choked me and my head popped up. I needed to keep my head under, but my body fought against what I wanted it to do. I waited where I sat and coughed out what I swallowed. I put my face back under and tried to pinch out the burn in my nose, but blocking my air made one arm flail. Then the other turned loose and flapped. "Stop splashing," I said, but it didn't work. I rested.

The night before had been a deep dark night. Bailey Renfroe had waited at the foot of my bed, not saying a word. I told him that this misery is no more than a passing ghost and closed my eyes against seeing him. "I'll slip out of my skin and float away. Leave me be," I told him. Now, if I could float, I could turn over and watch the moon, then sink low into the water. That would be a kind thing.

In the distance, I heard hoofbeats against the hard ground, followed by M'dear's call. I put my face back in the water and tried to kick out my legs so I could lay flat. With nothing to hold me up, I thought I would sink. M'dear and Hazel shouldn't see me like this. My knees scraped the bottom of the pond. I sat once more. When air hit my face, I cried.

M'dear waded out to me, making all kinds of splashing noises. Hazel followed with Ruby trotting behind, trying to keep up.

M'dear lifted me into her arms. She told me later I was no more than a puff of dry dandelion, even sopping wet. She staggered against the water's power, back to the bank, and laid me on the ground. I turned on my belly and sobbed. "Let me go, M'dear," I begged. "Please let me go."

Hazel nudged my foot with her nose. M'dear kneeled beside me and stroked my back, mumbling, "Baby, come on. Come back to your mama."

Chapter 32

Bailey Renfroe came in the early morning hours after M'dear took me from the pond. At first, I had mistrusted Bailey Renfroe's showing up a spirit. I thought he would fade in the light, but he always stayed.

"Hey, Odom."

"Bailey Renfroe, what you doing here?" I said that, but I wasn't surprised he was there. Bailey Renfroe always appeared when I needed him.

"Get out of bed, Odom. It's a bright blue morning."

"You still dead?"

"Sorta."

"My daddy talked to dead people. He talked to his dead mama at our house the night he left. You think I'm like my daddy?"

"I don't know your daddy. You going back to the pond?"

"Don't stand over there. Sit by me, here, on the edge of the bed." I patted the sheet.

"Ain't you scared?"

"Naw. I been to the pond."

"I know stuff," he said.

"Like what?"

"Miss Ophelia's setting outside your door, so's you don't go back to the pond. Mr. Walter's at his regular place on the porch, so's you don't go out through the treehouse. Miss Claire's going to Atlanta tomorrow to tell what they've give you at the clinic, but she don't know it yet."

"Where's Brother Blues?"

"Closed up in his house, pining away." He sat on the bed. "You going back to the pond?"

"Naw. Oh, I don't know. Maybe. I'm so tired and sad. I want to curl up and sleep."

"It's what doctors call . . . what is it? 'De-pression.'"

"Mr. Walter asked M'dear to leave with him, and she turned him down. Because of me. I disappoint everybody every way I turn. I hurt M'dear. I hate myself."

"What they call 'suicidal.'"

"How you know all this?"

"Been 'round since I last saw you."

"You been *round* forever, Bailey Renfroe," I said, trying to smile.

He giggled.

"Will you be my best friend?" I asked.

"Already am. Pinky promise."

"Can I go with you?" I reached out my hand. "We can spend our days flitting around."

"No. Not now you can't."

"I wish I was with you. Patsy and Nell was out for me that day in the hall. But I guess you know that, too."

"Yes, I know."

Living with Brother Blues and spying around, Bailey Renfroe sure knew a lot. I was so tired, I drifted off without seeing him leave. I laid bone straight so I wouldn't hurt. It made me stiff and rendered getting up hard, but getting up was hard anyway.

And he left. With him gone, I realized I should be shamed for him seeing me in my night clothes, but I wasn't. Wasn't shamed by my straight hair, my sores, my weeping abscess on my jaw. Wasn't shamed by not being able to cope with Nell Hawkins and her kind. I was just me and that was all.

Chapter 33

Summer was almost a month over, and it still hadn't rained. I was getting used to the sores, but I missed the mud and dry leaves of my run-away day. That mud had relieved the throbs. The sores, they started to heal now that I didn't go to the clinic. I didn't go back to school.

The first week of fall, I sat high in my chinaberry tree, trying to catch a breeze. So far, none come by. In the distance, Mr. Walter – that's what he's asked me to call him after he found me on the road – Mr. Walter herded a few cows toward the barn for hay. A dark, damp trail followed his truck from where water sloshed out. Mr. Walter drove caterpillar-slow so as not to stir up dust on his herd. They followed the truck, little babies to their mamas' teats.

Over toward the highway to Montgomery, blackish clouds cut the sky in halves. Their darkness weakened what lay beneath them, washing out the blue. M'dear believes a sky that looks half-black, half-white carries rain and hard winds and cooler weather. So long with no rain, I didn't worry about being in the tree. I didn't expect rain today. If it came, I could drop down a limb or two and scooch through my window in a flash.

From under the bank of clouds, a heavy black car, biggest I ever saw, come down the road, kicking up a wall of dirt. Easing along, Miss Claire drove her old farm truck. Both car and truck stopped at the cattle grate.

Miss Claire jumped out first, wearing jeans and a faded Roll Tide tee-shirt. Her ragged tennis shoes, now dusty tan rather than white, flopped against her feet for lack of strings as she passed the car and bounded up on the porch. I dropped three limbs down and slid into my treehouse for a better listen. Miss Claire hugged M'dear. She talked so fast, I couldn't understand what she said. M'dear cocked her head and narrowed her eyes. Not so sure herself, I could tell.

Three men dressed in black suits walked toward the porch. A woman in a straight-skirt suit followed them. She could have been Miss Claire the first day she had come back in July, only she was colored. The woman had trouble watching her step for patties while trying to see if she'd be attacked by a cow. Before she reached the inner gate, Hazel trotted up and nuzzled her from behind. The woman squealed the type of stepped-on-squeal a pup would make. I sniggered behind my hand. The men ignored her and moved on together shoulder-to-shoulder, as if they walked through cow pastures every day.

Here were these strangers Miss Claire had brought to our house. I know how M'dear felt about strangers. They're not to be trusted. Give her Brother Blues or Mr. Walter, she's alright. It took some talkings together to get her to trust Miss Claire. And now she'd brought in four citified coloreds, right to our front porch.

Miss Claire had such a proud grin across her face she could've been named Harvest Queen.

M'dear stared at the people, ready to defend me and her from attack. "Why you show up here with these town strangers?" she said. "Ain't I carrying burden enough without you adding more?" M'dear's face's crunched into her mad look, but I could tell she was scared by the way she opened and closed her left hand, rolling her fingers into a fist. But M'dear hurt, too. Hurt enough to let tears drop on her purple, floweredy housedress.

Miss Claire reached to put her arm across M'dear's shoulder, but M'dear stepped back. Miss Claire bowed her head. You would've thought M'dear had slapped her face. "I told you I quit the clinic. I told you what the shots were and what they were for. I'm trying to help undo what I've done."

By now, I felt my own tears. Strange how I could miss something I never had. I remembered Miss Claire holding me after the wreck. Except M'dear, she's the only person who has touched me since I couldn't remember. Patsy Green pulling my hair didn't count. I needed to get out of my treehouse and give her a hug. But I held my peace. A good spy don't give herself away.

The men were at the steps. The woman lagged behind to be sure the inner gate was latched. Hazel stood on the other side, shaking her big box head. Not used to being locked out, not her.

"Please," Miss Claire pleaded. She raised her voice, not talking quiet anymore. "Let me do what's decent."

M'dear's face dropped and dropped some more. She gazed down. She could've been a stray that had killed the best laying hen, scared and guilty all at the same time. "Got my own burden to bear in this." She waited a thinking minute. "I'll listen, but they can't come in my house."

About this time, Mr. Walter and Brother Blues walked around the corner of the house and up the porch. There stood my family all in a row. I smiled. Somebody should've took a picture.

Miss Claire stepped out of the line, but she took M'dear's hand. For her or for M'dear, I don't know. "I asked these people here today. They're with the SCLC, the Southern Christian Leadership Council in Atlanta. They're here to talk about the clinic."

I swallowed hard. That would mean me. I leaned closer to my door.

M'dear opened the screen door. "Come in and have a seat in our living room." She turned toward where I hid. "Margaret Ann Odom!" she called. "Get down out that treehouse. I know you're there. Company's here."

By the time I stepped inside, Miss Claire had brought in three kitchen chairs and had everybody sitting in a circle. I went over, stood behind her and placed my hands on her shoulders. Bailey Renfroe lingered over by the kitchen door, holding a fistful of hyssop blooming like crazy.

The rest of the afternoon gave up to my family's stories, all told out loud. M'dear and her misguided need to lift me higher than my chinaberry tree. Brother Blues and his belief in M'dear's goodness. Miss Claire and her trips to Montgomery to find what the shot medicine was, and the attack by the "esteemed Dr. Graves" when she quit the clinic. And Mr. Walter. He spoke with a heaviness in his voice put there by this burden he carried but never spoke of. Mr. Walter, who had known my daddy, the wealthy Hank Bullard, owned the clinic but hadn't spoke it for fear of losing his job.

M'dear sobbed out her grief—for my daddy and for Mr. Walter. It was like somebody had died.

Me? I didn't tell my story. No need to. I had lived it.

Chapter 34

The trial didn't appear on the docket until six years later, July, 1974. Several weeks earlier, M'dear got a subpoena from the prosecution. It told her to appear in the US Federal Court July 23, 1974 to testify about what happened to me the summer of 1968. So much time had passed since then that M'dear had given up any chance of Hank Bullard facing justice.

Yet there was the letter, snug inside her purse. The mail carrier his own self had handed it to her. As soon as the dust settled behind him, she put on her flip-flops and we walked up the road to Blues Marshall's store so he could read the words to her. The Southern Poverty Law Center was charging the Free Women's Clinic of using federal funds to experiment on and sterilize young Black girls. M'dear had to testify because she had agreed to let me receive treatments at the clinic.

"Blues, what I gone and done? This should've been over and done with," M'dear said. She dropped into a slat-bottomed chair and wrapped her legs around the supports. All the time, she wrung her hands.

Blues kneeled before her and clasped her hands. "We get this done, and we be fine."

"I ain't going." M'dear shook her head. "No telling what he might do."

"Yes, you going." Blues told her. "The law say you got to. You just step your fine self up on that big dog bus and ride away from here."

Pain of knowing that Brother Blues wanted her to leave Hyssop and me showed on her face as clear as the pain when she learned that I had been an experiment in my own daddy's clinic.

"I ain't never been on no Greyhound Bus. I ain't never been nowhere since he brought me here. I don't want to go nowhere else." M'dear pleaded as she looked into Blues' eyes.

"Oh, you come back. You come back strong and free of this burden you done been carrying,"

Blues assured her. "He got to abide the law just like you and me."

The day M'dear caught the bus, she left me with Brother Blues. He told her she didn't have to sit in the back, that she didn't have to think that way. But once she stepped into the aisle and looked down the two rows of seats, she must have known. I watched through the little square windows as she walked the aisle. She straightened her shoulders, clutched her pocketbook, and kept her eyes straight ahead. She did not look at a single face, but she must have felt pairs of eyes sizing her up and down with every step. She paused then sat gently into the corner of the bench seat. She waved a tiny wave to me and Brother Blues from the backseat of the big dog bus. A somewhat-smile made it across her face. We smiled back at her.

There's ongoing judgment amongst people. In your mind, you may ask why M'dear sent me to the clinic if she really had my best interest at heart. Times, they was different. You need to understand M'dear's life. In M'dear's world, White people provided.

Claire Whitehurst and me, we grew up in different worlds: hers, White; mine, Black. I never heard Miss Claire call us trash, but one look at how we lived would have set her thinking. I do believe she changed. She did come to repent to M'dear about what happened to me, but after it was all over, she disappeared. Brother Blues, who knows more than most of us, said she moved to Arizona to work with the Navajo. Maybe she felt as out of place in our world as I felt at the clinic and the colored school.

After the trial, M'dear and Brother Blues sent me to live with his sister Paulette in Cincinnati. I got a job at a big library and read myself into a world of knowing. And I didn't try to pass as White. I was who I was.

Some things stay with you. Like fear. Fear lasts our whole lifetime, even if we hide it. I don't have a fear of living out here by myself, but I fear that nobody will love me since I lost M'dear and Mr. Walter. Real fear. I've held the pain it brought close to my chest. I oftentimes tell myself "this is mine." I accept it. This feeling of not belonging. It's one of the few things I have left of my growing up.

There was no payout for what happened to me. I guess even judges know you can't put a price on taking part of a person's soul. I didn't undergo any sterilization surgeries like some girls had, I later found out. But the injections had done enough damage. Even if I had gotten married, I could never have had a child of my own.

During those years away, I came to know that what was done to me wasn't done in the interest of helping people. It was done to see that no vestige of Margaret Ann Odom would live on after me. I was a second-class citizen. Alabama didn't need any more of me. What had happened come about in a time of not knowing, a time when doctors thought it would be better not to upset patients. So they didn't tell them the truth. They didn't say nothing, and us coloreds, we didn't ask nothing. We were all wrong. I was wrong for hiding my pain, M'dear was wrong for not questioning what was happening to me, and the doctors, nurses, and other people who had tricked us were wrong for a whole world of reasons.

Maybe it's true that I'll never amount to much, old as I am, but if this hadn't happened to me, maybe my children or grandchildren or even great-grandchildren would have. I will never know. Where would the world be if they had sterilized Reverend King's mother? You can never know what a person will grow up to be until they get there. I can respect science and medicine and doctors, but I can respect honoring people for who we are as well.

In the late 1960s, nobody in Hyssop had ever heard of the Tuskegee experiments on Black men who had syphilis. Most of them had already died. To get rid of us coloreds, they tried to force sterilization on us. After all my studying in Cincinnati, I now know it had been going on for generations, quiet-like and secret. Nobody had heard about the Mississippi appendectomies that were actually hysterectomies done on poor Black women and girls. Me, I believe that's what caused Bella Whitstone's girl to bleed to death, but like I said before, nobody asked me.

A person's not like hyssop. Hyssop will grow back and bloom in its own time, not so with taking away the power of a person's body. That's permanent. Makes a ghost of a person in a way. I'm finally settled with the knowing of what was done to me. Nowadays, I can tell the what, but I ponder the why of it all every day.

Afterword

In 1973, Southern Poverty Law Center (SPLC) brought charges against the Family Planning Clinic of the Montgomery Community Action Committee, which was funded and controlled at the federal level for misrepresenting "investigational drugs." Given that two African-American girls, Minnie Lee (12) and Mary Alice Relf (14), were involved, charges included "insertion of a dangerous type of IUD (intra-uterine device)" and "surgical sterilization without their mother's permission or knowledge." Mrs. Relf, who could neither read nor write, put an "X" on a consent form without details on the nature of the surgical procedure being provided (Relf vs. Weinberger 1974). The Court ruled that the "agency sought out the Relf children as good experimental subjects for their family planning Program." No complaints were filed against any individual. The Court ruled that federally assisted family planning sterilizations are permissible only with the voluntary, knowing and uncoerced consent of individuals competent to give such consent.[1]

---

1. http://www.racismreview.com/blog/2007/09/22/sterilization-and-women-of-color/

Discussion Questions

1. Discuss the title of the novel and its significance. What role does the drought play in the story?

2. The setting has a direct impact on making Margaret Ann susceptible to Dr. Grave's experiments. How might she have been less vulnerable had she lived in a less rural location?

3. Hyssop is a plant that has been used for healing as far back as Biblical times. Find references to hyssop in the novel. What is the significance of all the hyssop dying during the drought?

4. The medicine Margaret Ann is given causes her to become more depressed as the story progresses. In what ways is her depression evident to the reader?

5. Why do you think Margaret Ann stays silent about how her body is being affected by the shots?

6. Margaret Ann treats Ruby as her baby. She also has Baa, her worn lamb that she cuddles. How do these two relate to Margaret Ann and the clinic's plan to prevent her from later in life becoming a mother?

7. Margaret Ann's mother, Ophelia Odom, refuses to report what happens at the clinic after Miss Claire tells her the truth. Ophelia gives reasons for not standing up against the White establishment. For what other reasons might Ophelia take this stand?

8. How did you feel about Walter Gibbons after learning that he knew Margaret Ann's father owns the Free Women's Clinic?

9. Having no knowledge of eugenics leads Margaret Ann to misunderstand the term and say she has "blue jennies." What other examples of miscommunications occur in the story and how do these misunderstandings reinforce the innocence of the children?

10. Why is secrecy necessary for the clinic to carry out its experiments?

11. Which character, if any, seems to be most responsible for what happens to Margaret Ann?

12. This story is based on an actual court case. The characters and setting are fiction and are not intended to represent any individual living or dead, nor any particular location. The decision handed down by the U.S. Supreme Court is printed at the end of the novella. Knowing this decision, how do you feel about the Southern Poverty Law Center taking this issue to court?

CPSIA information can be obtained
at www.ICGtesting.com
Printed in the USA
LVHW090725120222
710987LV00005B/65

9 781949 711820